THE ENTIRE GOAT

(ENTRAILS INCLUDED)

THE ENTIRE GOAT (ENTRAILS INCLUDED)

A Collection of Short Horrors

ANTON BRINZA

Cover illustrations: Gyubin Song
Cover design: Arturo Palomo

ISBN 979-8-9915061-3-7 (ebook)
ISBN 979-8-9915061-4-4 (print)

Published by
LUDOVICO TREATS PUBLISHING LLC
www.ludovicotreats.com
www.antonbrinza.com

Dedicated to
the woman who let me
watch horror films as a child

Have a scream, Mom

A NOTE TO READERS

The first five stories in this collection have been released as a free ebook called *Half the Goat,* available through the Ludovico Treats website. If you have purchased this volume after reading that set, I'd like to thank you for sticking with it and coming along on this journey with me. If you have, on the other hand, come straight to this book, I want to express equal thanks and also encourage you to head to the website for your free half-volume anyway. You can keep it for your collection or pass it along to another lover of horror fiction. Perhaps you could gift it to someone who has expressed an interest in horror but doesn't quite have the stomach for it. Tell them it's only "half as scary," which would not technically be a lie but only a slight untruth. Maybe you'd prefer to use it as a sleep palliative, a meditation talisman, or a coaster (just don't blame me for damage to your digital device.) The point is, it's free, and everyone deserves free goat parts. Do anything you like with it, but whatever you do, please enjoy *The Entire Goat (Entrails Included)* and... Do not mistreat the goat!

CONTENTS

"Never enter a forest
without knowledge of the trails."

ONE FINAL TRICK

The gun-metal blue Buick LeSabre had been following her since the Pennsylvania border. Three hours already, maybe longer. She knew it was foolish to think so, but it seemed impossible to believe that it was not in some way connected to what happened at the park.

Though she could not explain it, she could pinpoint the moment it started. Inexplicably, something had changed. An invisible shawl had been draped over the world as Maggie Garrick knew it. Ever since, it just kept wrapping tighter, squeezing her, changing her, manipulating her in a way she could not control. If she didn't find a way to stop or escape it, pretty soon she would emerge from this cocoon—transformed into something unrecognizable. Something horrid.

It got so bad that she had to leave home. Didn't know where to go or if she'd ever come back or even if it would help, but everything else she tried only made it worse. So, she got into her car and drove.

She'd been on the road for over ten hours, driving an aimless, wandering route with no destination in mind. After crossing four state borders, she hoped something would have changed, but nothing had. It only got worse.

If asked what was wrong—as several people had over the past couple of days—Maggie could not explain what she felt. Did she feel ill? No. Was she under stress? No more than usual. Had someone or something spooked her? Not exactly. Was she paranoid? That was closer to the truth, but no. Had she done something wrong? Broken the law? Slept with someone she shouldn't have? Smoked too much grass? No, no, no, and no.

The best way she could have described it, had she tried, might have been to say that beginning four days ago at precisely 11:44 a.m., while sitting on a park bench in her home-town of Mount Airy, Maryland, she had experienced a sudden and unexplained sense of dread. Nothing noticeable had taken place. People walked their dogs. Mothers pushed their babies in strollers. A couple sat on the next bench over, holding hands. A group of teens was throwing a Frisbee. A young man was taking pictures with his phone. A father was helping his daughter get her kite airborne. The weather had been lovely, perfect for a day off work. Life seemed just fine and dandy, perhaps too perfect. And then a dark pall had settled over her.

Maggie's best friend, Cindy Weir, sometimes suffered severe panic attacks. Cindy had described these attacks to Maggie often enough, so she initially thought she was experiencing something similar. But Maggie had never dealt with any sort of anxiety before. Then, she thought it might be an allergic reaction. However, she had no physical symptoms whatsoever—none but the weight of the world itself constricting around her.

That was then. Now, the physical effects were undeniable. Her heart had sped up crazily and felt ready to blow. It had been thudding double-time since passing through West Virginia's northern panhandle, when she first noticed that

Buick following her. Her mind had been spinning like a carnival ride since leaving Maryland. Every face she saw looked wrong somehow. Immoral. Every object seemed misplaced or broken or diseased. She wanted to avoid others and also claw at them, begging for help. Her limbs felt disconnected, and her eyes looked like someone else's staring back at her through the rearview mirror.

Maggie prayed she could find a private place—an abandoned house, a hotel with no guests, a secluded cabin in the woods, a boat to take out on one of the Great Lakes—someplace, anyplace where she could just lie down and let this pass. She had already accepted what letting it pass truly meant. Either these feelings would sort themselves out, or she'd fall unconscious from the stress and never wake up.

Hopefully.

Hopefully, it would be that easy. She did not possess the kind of courage she would need to off herself—never had before, and definitely not now. She could barely look at her own reflection without feeling a stab of fear.

A boat would be best, but that meant she needed to figure out where the hell she was so she could start heading north. Eventually, she would run into Lake Erie.

But what about this car that was following her? The two guys inside looked like fucking creeps. A couple of times, they'd pulled up right alongside her. Though she had kept her gaze trained on the road ahead, she felt their leering, depraved eyes. It was insane, but she imagined she could smell their predatory intentions. When she sped up, they fell behind, and then they would appear on her tail again fifty miles later as though they'd never left. She got off the freeway to grab a burger from a drive-thru, and they pulled into the same fast food joint while she was waiting for her food. They went inside to eat, but she could have sworn they were watching her from their window seat as she drove off. From that point, she avoided the highways, sticking to the local roads. Still, half an hour later, she saw them gaining on her again. They'd already trailed her damn near across Ohio. Say she made a turn to head north now, at some arbitrary road out in the middle of nowhere, and they *kept* following her—then at least she'd know she wasn't imagining it. That would be the first reassuring sign since this mental breakdown began.

Was it really a breakdown, though?

It felt more like...like a curse. Like someone had bound her soul with rough twine so they could drag it out of her. But why would someone curse her? What had she done to deserve it? Who would do something like that? And—what the fuck?— what kind of moron believed in curses anyhow? It didn't make sense. It was absurd. And yet, the more she considered it, the more certain she became. That was precisely what had happened. That day in the park, someone, for some reason, had hexed her. And it actually worked.

Why her? Maggie Garrick lived a slow, almost dull life. Her group of friends was small and tight-knit. Most of them went to church every Sunday. She got along with her parents and coworkers. She didn't have any debt or legal troubles. The last person she'd hurt was an ex-boyfriend, but that happened ten years ago after they had already drifted apart. As far as she knew, he was married and living in another country. So why did she feel like someone had started jabbing needles into a voodoo doll in her likeness?

An Exxon filling station appeared on the right. Maggie thought about stopping to rest. She was tired of driving. She could use the restroom and also ask about the fastest route to Lake Erie. At the moment, the Buick was not riding her ass. A pair of headlights shone at a distance, just tiny glimmers in the rearview, but she did not doubt it was that same car. If she stopped, it would have to be somewhere with plenty of people. Witnesses.

Before she even reached the Exxon, she saw how dimly lit and empty it was. No other cars. Probably only a single attendant who might be just as creepy as these assholes following her. Nothing short of an empty tank could compel her to stop here. The best thing to do would be to step on the gas, get as far ahead as possible, and then make that turn at the next crossroads.

Maggie pressed down on the accelerator. The speedometer jumped to seventy, then seventy-five, and slowly crawled past eighty. Plenty over the speed limit. The lights of the Exxon station fell away behind her, and the distant headlights grew fainter. Though the road was straight, it was entirely without streetlights, so she needed to keep her eyes on the lane. Still, she found it difficult to tear her eyes from the rearview. Finally, she let out a deep breath when the headlights slowed and turned into the filling station.

At least, she thought they did. She didn't see them in the rearview anymore, but she was already second-guessing herself. Did she really see them slow down and turn? Had they simply fallen behind again? Maybe she'd gone over a slight rise in the road that the other car had yet to mount. And, she could not discount the thought that she had imagined the whole thing.

Her breath rasped, harsh and heavy. She kept telling herself to stick to the plan—keep going, keep up the speed, follow the road until the next right turn. With any luck, she wouldn't blow past a cop. Actually, maybe that would be best. If a cop pulled her over, those stalkers would have no choice but to leave her alone.

She continued staring into the rearview, trying to decide whether she saw the subtle glow of headlights. After a while, two tiny flecks of light appeared. If they were headlights, they were far behind her but probably close enough to see her turn off the road. It occurred to her that they could switch off their headlights. If they did, they could get a lot closer without her even realizing it. What if they already had? What if that faint light was the sick glow of the dashboard lights illuminating their pale, lecherous faces? The gleam of their stained teeth?

Her mind felt clouded and doubtful, like someone standing at a high ledge, intending to jump but not sure why. The disturbing awareness of being followed made her distracted and jumpy. She knew she'd been too focused on the rearview, but she thought she'd been paying good enough attention to the road ahead. However, by the time she saw the person in the middle of the lane, it was too late.

The next few seconds progressed so quickly that Maggie could not be sure of exactly what happened.

Slamming on the brakes did not stop her from hitting the pedestrian at nearly full speed. Her Ford Taurus skidded another fifty yards, dragging the body along the road beneath her front bumper. Fortunately, she had been sensible enough not to swerve and run into the ditch. Her car stopped somewhat askew but still in the lane. A splatter of blood lay across the hood.

For an entire minute—maybe two—she listened to her own hoarse breathing and felt her pulse all throughout her body. Her mind, on the other hand, felt clear for the first time since the park. Although she knew she'd just hit and most likely killed someone, that sense of paranoia and dread had paradoxically lifted.

But her relief was short-lived. The ominous sense of foreboding returned like a slow, lurching cloud, and now it was worse. The world went dark around Maggie. She saw nothing but the spray of her headlights on the asphalt, the left one giving off a ruddy glow. Bits and pieces of memory flashed before her eyes, the instant before the collision not quite syncing with reality.

First of all, based on the suit and white shirt, she was sure it had been a man. But he looked rather feminine. Asian, maybe. Then, there was his expression—his eyes had been open and alert, but he did not appear shocked to see an automobile bearing down on him. Instead, he had a look of... Ecstasy? Rapture? And finally, Maggie would swear that he had not been standing in the lane when she hit him—he had been horizontal. Not falling from the sky horizontal, but suspended in the air. Just hanging there, a few feet off the ground.

In one sense, Maggie knew those fragmentary memories could not possibly be true. And yet, nothing had made much sense over the past few days. Nothing at all. So, this accident, occurring in this implausible fashion, almost seemed like the only thing that could have happened. Like it was fated. Or controlled.

Maggie put the car in park and cracked the door open, not getting out right away but only considering what to do. She had hit the man at such a frightening speed. What would she find? What would be left of him? The blood on the hood shined like an oil slick in the dim moonlight. Knowing what she had just done to another person was bad enough, but if she got out and saw a disfigured, lacerated body, she was sure it would tip her right over the edge. But what else could she do?

Just keep driving, honey. They're coming.

The voice formulated in her mind and sounded like her, but it came from somewhere else. Or someone else. It came from the awful, depressing, persecutory feeling she'd been besieged by. And though it was sensible advice, she ignored it, perhaps out of defiance or perhaps because no matter how removed from reality she was, she still contained a shred of humanity.

Pushing the door open, Maggie stepped out into the cool

night. Unconsciously, she arched her back and stretched her legs. It was the first time she'd gotten out since the Buick started trailing her. Avoiding the gruesome sight in front of her car as long as possible, she stared back along the road. The lights of the Exxon station were no longer visible. She peered into the darkness and thought she saw a blur of motion. Again, she heard that voice telling her to *Keep driving, honey,* because it wouldn't take that Buick long to catch up. Unless she intended to give them a welcome party, she needed to keep moving.

But what if the man who'd jumped or fallen in front of her car wasn't dead?

Jumped? Fallen? No...that couldn't be right. Glancing around, she saw an open stretch of road. There was no place to jump from. No trees, towers, or power lines. With each passing second, the image formed more vividly in her mind—he hadn't been falling; he had been suspended in mid-air. She was sure of it.

Squinting behind her, she felt like she was praying to see a pair of headlights. She knew they were there. They had to be because she couldn't handle these mind games anymore. She didn't want to face any more questions about what was real and what wasn't. No matter how hard she stared or how many times she rubbed her eyes, she saw no lights approaching.

With the car still running, Maggie stepped around to the front and gasped.

The man lay splayed on the concrete, his limbs shattered and bent unnaturally. Half of his face had been crushed. Bits of skull and brain matter clung to the Taurus's grill. The other half of his face was severely scratched and bruised but still showed that look of bliss she'd seen in the moment before impact. A substance that looked like vomit clung to his chin and collar, and he did not appear to be breathing.

Maggie didn't breathe either. She held her breath, staring at the mangled body. Twelve hours earlier, she was at home—

she'd felt like she was losing her mind then, too, but at least she was someplace safe. Now she was lost in the middle of Bumblefuck, Ohio, and she'd just killed a man who she would swear had been floating above the road. Everything about it pointed to a total separation from reality. Everything except the fact that she was aware of it. If she'd really lost a grip, would she know it? Was that how it happened? Did people know when they were going insane?

A noise alerted her, tearing her out of her thoughts and back to the macabre sight lying in the spray of her headlights. It sounded like a low moan. Maggie stepped closer to the body and bent over the man's maimed face. If he was making that sound, he did it without moving his lips or his broken jaw.

The sound grew louder, a low thrumming sound coming not from the man but from the road.

Maggie's eyes bulged from their sockets, and her breath hitched again when she recognized the roar of an engine.

She stayed down, crouching behind her front fender as she peered around the open driver's side door. A pair of headlights was coming toward her and moving fast.

Her first instinct was to get back in the car and peel out of there. Either that or wait and pray that it was not the Buick but rather someone who could help.

Acting on instinct, she started to crawl toward the door but felt something on her ankle. She looked down and blared a shrill scream into the silent darkness of the surrounding fields.

The man's bloody, disfigured hand was wrapped around her ankle. It tugged weakly but persistently. She kicked it off and stumbled backward, slamming her shoulders into the bumper and rubbing her neck in the slick warmth of blood. Skittering out of the man's reach, she stepped on his groin, her hands swiping through the blood on the hood as she tried to right herself. She tripped and fell on her ass, scraping her palms in the gravel of the roadside. The revving of the oncoming engine grew louder. She could now see the car's shape and recognized it at once. They were still coming for her. When she glanced back at the bloodied body, she saw it moving. It was no longer reaching for her and clearly not struggling to hold onto life; instead, it rose as though a magnet was slowly lifting it off the ground. The body hovered limply two feet above the road, exactly as when she hit the guy.

Maggie tried to scream again, but no sound emerged. The Buick was speeding closer. It would reach her in a matter of seconds. And now this corpse was actually floating in the light of her headlights, just inches from her face. She could reach out and touch him, drag him back to the ground if she wanted to.

She did not want that. All she wanted was an end to this madness.

Staying low, Maggie crab-walked off the road, dipping into the shallow, soggy ditch below the shoulder. She turned and scrambled across to the weedy growth on the other side, crawling into the grass as far as she could until she heard the Buick skid to a stop behind her car.

Flattened out and peeking through the grass, she had a sight on both cars. Though she was concealed, she felt exposed. The dead man hovered in the air, rising higher.

Two doors creaked open, and two obnoxious male voices immediately filled the air. She couldn't hear what they were saying, but she knew they were talking about her. They bent down, peering in through her Taurus's rear window. When they came astride the rear doors, they both stopped. The man on the passenger side abruptly stood rigid, pointing at the levitating body. Blood dripped from the gaping wound in the dead man's face, splattering the concrete. The body rose higher still, not by its own volition but rather like an invisible rope was wrapped around its waist, dangling it with purpose.

Bait, thought Maggie.

The two men laughed and cursed in disbelief but kept stepping closer. The one coming up along the driver's side stopped at the open door and poked his head into her car. Their energy became more urgent; their voices grew louder.

"Where the fuck did she go?"

"Where do you think?" said the other. "She just killed this guy!"

"Good. Then we won't have to feel bad for what we're about to do to her."

"But how do you explain this? Is there something wrong with my eyes? That dead guy's floating, right? Right?"

"I don't give a shit about some dead Chinaman. I want the girl. Find her."

"How's it possible? She must be toying with us. I told you she saw us..."

"So what if the bitch saw us? What's she gonna do?" snarled the man on the driver's side, waving something around that looked like a gun. Or a hammer.

"Don't you see this shit? That guy's flying! She's not a bitch, she's a fucking witch! Come on, Travis. I think we need to get outta here—"

"Shut up, you spineless immigrant shit! Listen! Did you hear that?"

"Hear what?"

"There. Shh."

The man believed he had heard Maggie, but he spun toward the opposite side of the road. Maggie had also heard the sound. Gazing up and down the road, she saw nothing but sank further into the grass. Whatever the noise was, it did not sound friendly. The man who heard it raised his weapon and stalked the opposite shoulder while his buddy stepped forward to examine the battered, hovering body. The sound grew louder—a complex, layered sound consisting of whooshing, growling, and tearing—and Maggie realized it was not coming from across the road.

It was coming from above.

The hair on her arms stood up. She felt a presence that did not belong. When she looked up, she saw nothing in the sky, but in the same way that she had sensed a slow dread coiling around her the past four days, she sensed something in the sky now. Somehow, she knew it was alive but not organic. Extraterrestrials? Sentient drones? Demonic spirits? She didn't think any of these were quite right, but just as with the idea of a curse, she could not deny that something unfathomable was happening. And she didn't want anything to do with it. Even witnessing it from the periphery was too close.

"Look!" shouted one of the men, pointing at the sky.

As soon as Maggie heard the first gunshot, she started running. Not bothering to crouch anymore, she took off, oblivious to which direction she headed as long as she escaped the mayhem that had just begun.

Though she didn't look back, she knew they weren't shooting at her. They might have found her, but they'd been distracted by the floating corpse and the ghastly sound emitting from above. They never even had the chance to search for her before the man started firing at...

At what? Maggie had heard it, too. She had felt something nearby. But she hadn't seen anything. Maybe it really was all in her head. Panic and hysteria had finally drowned her mind, shrouding her life in darkness and delirium. Or, maybe they were shooting at her. She hardly had the sense to tell the difference anymore.

Her legs carried her away automatically, her mind stunted in dumb shock like a blackout bag had been stuffed over her head. She stumbled through the grass and weeds until she was far enough behind the cars to limp onto the road, where she could run faster. Without realizing it, she was headed back toward the filling station.

She glanced over her shoulder only once. An unnatural

blackness hovered above the two cars. She saw it but didn't register it—her entire life had come to resemble that darkness. It repelled her, of course, but it had come to feel almost natural.

By the time she reached the Exxon, her mind was so addled with paranoia that she thought the best course of action might be to douse herself in gasoline and set herself alight. But what was she going to do? Barge into the shop and buy a fucking Bic? Ask the clerk to come out and torch her next to the pumps because she was too faint-hearted to do it herself?

The clerk sat inside with his eyes closed, though it didn't look like he was sleeping. Jerking himself off, maybe. Either way, he didn't notice Maggie racing around the side of the building. She prayed that the restrooms were unlocked and became tense when she saw yellow tape stretched across the men's room door, with a sign reading *Out of Order*. The ladies' room, however, was unobstructed and unlocked. Once inside, she discovered that there was no lock on the door at all, which did not bode well. She didn't intend to spend the night, of course, but she would have liked a few minutes of relative security to gather her wits. Without any idea what she would do, she leaned against the door and tried to catch her breath. Her skin crawled at the sight of the dingy bathroom. She needed her car, but how could she trust it was safe to return? As much as she hated to admit it, what she needed most was a police station. She had no recollection of the last town she'd passed through, so continuing on foot wouldn't do any good. Maybe she would have no choice but to hunker down here. The clerk could call the cops. But what would she tell them when they showed up? What would they do when they saw the body in the road with half its skull plastering the front of her car?

How would she ever make it to Lake Erie if she was detained on manslaughter charges? And then, what would the curse do to her if she was cooped up in a prison cell?

The bathroom had two stalls on the right and two sinks to the left. The first sink had a busted faucet, so Maggie stepped up to the second sink. She twisted the knob and shoved her hands into the icy water. Her reflection in the grimy mirror made her shudder in disgust. She hadn't realized how awful she looked. Her hair was wild and unwashed, her eyes bloodshot with heavy dark circles cradling them, and her skin wrinkled with the strain of constant disquiet.

Cupping her hands, she splashed water on her face, rubbing with excessive but necessary force. She wanted to wash away the past couple of days. Everything, starting with whatever just happened by the cars and all the way back to that innocent, uneventful day at the park. She would do anything to wipe it all out and return to her calm, peaceful, rote way of life. If she believed in such things, she would offer to sell her soul to have those days surgically removed, like cutting into the body to remove a diseased organ. And maybe she did believe. After all, if she believed in curses now, why not that?

She scrubbed harder, wishing she had a coarse sponge. The water stung her eyes. She squeezed them and pressed harder to get the water out, but her vision remained blurred. Blinking repeatedly, she looked up, focusing on the mirror. And she saw something there...but not what she expected.

After digging her palms into her eyes one more time, Maggie gazed into the mirror and realized her vision was fine. It wasn't her eyes. The bulbous, blurry form she saw was inside the mirror. It seemed like a physical manifestation of all the awful presentiments she'd lived with the past four days, giving shape to her chaotic feelings of panic and despair, reality dismantled into a vision of brutality and torture. Without understanding why or how, Maggie saw that she had been thrust into a deadly game of cat and mouse, set into a labyrinth designed by a brilliant lunatic. She was not the only one, but just a single chess piece nudged around a crowded game board, where her every action would have consequences that caused pain and suffering to herself and others. Visions of torture and death swam within the glass, affecting people she recognized and others she didn't. Herself. Her friends. An old woman. A man she'd seen on the news. An ex-boyfriend. She didn't want to look, but just like staring into the rearview, she could not look away.

A final chilling image rose before her. She saw her Taurus, the Buick that had been following her, and something that defied comprehension. A hoarse, grating breath emerged from her throat as she tried to scream. All at once, she saw that she had been right—those two men had been following her, and they meant to attack her. To torture her. But then she was shown what happened to those men after she ran away. Though she felt a momentary tickle of pleasure, she knew it didn't make sense. She decided none of what she was experiencing could be real. She must be in the midst of a nervous breakdown. There was no other way to explain it. She had lost her mind. The dread she'd been running from, the men in the Buick, the curse, the floating body, the visions in the mirror— all of it was nothing more than the withering of her mental faculties. It had to be...because believing anything else at this stage would drive her off the deep end anyway. She was stuck at a crossroads where all four directions led to the same destination.

Lifting her fists, Maggie finally released an unhinged shriek and threw her arms into the mirror. It shattered, slicing up her forearms as glass rained into the sink.

Still screaming, Maggie Garrick ran from the restroom. She ran past the shop window, startling the clerk, who was already on edge about the scream he'd just heard. He watched idiotically as she staggered around the fuel pumps before dashing into the field behind the building.

Maggie did not know which direction she was running. Two hundred and thirty miles lay between her and the shores of Lake Erie, a long way on foot. Even if she had known how far it was, she would not have stopped running. Her life had been reduced to this last desperate escape act. This was the final routine in a magician's stage show, and she was the assistant, drawn too tightly into the dark shawl of madness to ever be untangled.

APARTMENT 303

Describing a scream never does it justice, but that's what I heard. A single, blood-curdling scream in the middle of the night.

My wife was asleep beside me, and I was oh-so-close. Teetering on the brink. Floating on a raft down the lazy River Lethe, right at the curve where consciousness and slumber become indistinguishable.

Our building's walls keep out most of the sounds from the other apartments, but not everything. When Teddy Osmund in 201 broke a pitcher over his fiancé's head, Noreen Spinks from 203 heard it and called the cops. When my wife and I briefly tried to conceive a year ago, Mrs Lisotho down in 302 pestered us daily, saying, "You two lovebirds havin' any success yet, or just a lot of fun?"

As I lay in bed on the night of the scream, no sounds could be heard. Not a drip, a tick, or a tock. No TVs, no footsteps, no voices. Our window was cracked open, but even the general sounds of midnight traffic were fainter than usual. At intervals almost eerie in their precision, someone coughed outside, most likely our resident bum living in the alley. Other than that cough, it was dead silent.

If the scream had come ten seconds later, I might've slept through it. My mind would have cataloged it in the subconscious and worked it into the dreams that came later. Instead, the scream came before I passed that threshold, with the expected effect—it scared the ever-loving piss out of me. Not in the way you're gripped by fear if you hear someone breaking into your house, but more of an existential terror, as though you'd just seen a genuine ghost and could not comprehend.

My eyes shot open, staring into the darkness of our bedroom as my heart kicked into high gear. I could feel my pulse, the blood darting through my veins with violent thrusts. The scream was so loud that I initially thought it came from our living room. I leaned onto my elbows, staring out the bedroom door and realizing how ridiculous the notion was. How could someone have entered our apartment without me hearing? Unless I *had* fallen asleep...

If it hadn't come from our apartment, it must have come from below us. Apartment 303. All four floors in our building have the same layout, so Carolynn Cazares's bedroom is directly underneath ours. Without a doubt, it had to be that batty old broad.

I shouldn't be so harsh. Mrs Cazares is nice enough, just a bit quirky. She's never caused a problem for us. Kind of a space cadet sometimes, but that's it. Not the type to cause a disturbance in the night.

I waited, figuring a scream like that could not occur without eliciting a reaction. Like the aftershocks of an earthquake, I expected something to follow—another scream, pounding footsteps, shattering glass, a slamming door, an angry shout, even a gunshot, for Christ's sake—something had to come next. The sheets became damp with sweat as I waited. I felt so goddamn tense that I might as well have been restrained to the bed like a common asylum inmate. At one point, I reached out and shook my wife's shoulder.

"Whit. Hey, Whit!" I whispered.

"Stop it..."

"You hear that scream?"

"What? Let me slee...'

She fell asleep again before the words slurred from her mouth. But what about me? I needed to get some sleep, too. Like everyone else, I had to be at work in the morning. Instead, I lay there for half the night, listening to my heart pounding in my eardrums, expecting to hear crying or sirens or thunderous footfalls in the stairwell.

But nothing happened. After a while, the silence became more unnerving than the scream itself. A heavy, invasive silence. An empty sonic landscape in which the scream repeated over and over in my head. A man can only take so much before he starts to worry about the soundness of his mind. What the hell? Had I imagined it? Was I having auditory hallucinations? Was it me who screamed? Startled myself right out of a nightmare? If so, then I spooked myself right into a living nightmare for the rest of that night.

Striving to fall asleep, my thoughts kept ping-ponging back and forth in search of rationale. If the scream came from me, then I had to be losing my mind...but if it didn't, then shouldn't I be doing something? Should I go down and knock on Mrs Cazares's door? Bust it down? Call 911? Was she dying down there? I imagined a drawn-out, convoluted scenario in which she'd been the victim of a home invasion, awakened by a maniac standing over her bed and then blurting out that one suffocating scream before being gagged and bound, the intruder torturing her into giving up her bank account information. After that, naturally, he'd be on his way up to our apartment...because that's how terror-fueled panic attacks always pan out.

At a generous estimate, I'd say I got a combined two hours of sleep that night. I woke up every twenty minutes in a cold sweat, not from bad dreams but just the memory of that goddamn scream. At ten past eight, I finally crawled out of bed. Whitney was worried that I had a fever. She swore she hadn't heard a thing in the night and didn't even remember me trying to wake her up. On my way down the stairs, I thought about knocking on Mrs Cazares's door, but I knew I would be late for work if I stopped. In the lobby, I passed Henrick Lewiston and Sue Demarco, mumbling a hello as I blew past them. Just before the lobby door shut behind me, I heard Sue say something along the lines of, "Leave her alone, Henny. She's just a lonely old kook. Screaming don't hurt no one…"

Knowing that I wasn't the only one who heard the scream really put my mind at ease. Throughout the day, I kept thinking about my childish reaction in the night. The scream had a perfectly logical explanation—of course it did—but I'd let it infect my mind, keeping me awake with a collage of irrational delusions.

Propelled by coffee, energy drinks, and the increasingly amusing nature of my sleepless night, I managed to make it through the workday without dozing off. I stopped worrying about Mrs Cazares and the tremulous insecurities that had kept me awake. As the day wore on, I found it easier to laugh at my unfounded nighttime fears. I was no different from a kid staring wide-eyed and fearful into a dark closet or shivering from a sound at the windowpane. The only thing that continued to nag at me was the coughing from out in the alley —a grim, pestilential soundtrack to the whole episode.

Considering how tired I was, I left work in a much better mood. A day's reflection on the incident made me realize how silly I had acted. I knew I couldn't blame myself. I must have been in a half-aware state the entire night, never fully awake but strained with fatigue, lost in a realm where imagination takes the reins. The prospect of going home and getting a real night's sleep provided a lightness to my steps. I even stopped by the pharmacy on the way home to pick up some cough medicine for the homeless guy.

I hoped to find him in the alley so I could talk to him. I'd seen him a few times, as most of the tenants in our building had, but few had ever spoken to him. The stigma against homeless people, I guess. He looks young, probably early to mid-twenties, and I just wanted to hear his story. Maybe there was something I could do to help get him on his feet again. Weird as it sounds, the whole experience seemed to have made me more compassionate.

The guy wasn't around, but he had tucked his gear into a tiny covered landing leading to an unused basement entrance of the neighboring building. I left the cough medicine on the cardboard box he used for a bed.

Our superintendent saw me emerging from the alley.

"What you doin' back there?"

"Hey, Mr Lorenzo. I just wanted to see if I could talk to the guy. You know, see if he's alright."

"What for? Selling him junk?"

"No, but I bought some cough syrup for him. Didn't you hear him coughing last night?"

Mr Lorenzo snorted and glared at me skeptically. "He'll just trade it to some other bum for a fix. I wouldn't bother. I'll have him outta here soon enough."

"What do you mean? Where's he going to go?"

"I don't give a shit. He can go and live in a tree for all I care. Just not the trees in front of my building. I called the cops."

"About the scream?"

"What are you talking about?"

"That scream in the night. Mrs Cazares, I think. Wasn't it?"

Hearing that, he scowled and bared his teeth. I wasn't sure whether it was at me or the mention of the scream.

"Never mind," I said with a sheepish grin.

"I called to have 'em send someone to take care of that lowlife. Get'im outta here. But those fuckers told me they got better things to worry about. You believe that? I'll keep calling. If they don't send someone, I'll do it myself. Chase that filthy scrounger right outta here."

"Leave him alone, Mr Lorenzo. He's not hurting anyone."

"You're what's wrong with this country, you know that?" he grumbled as he opened the door to his apartment, 101. "Young folks and their bleeding hearts. Welfare's draining our pockets, and you just want to keep on giving handouts. Starts with cough syrup. Pretty soon, you'll be delivering smack. Goddamn hypodermic needles and whores and god knows what all. The keys to fucking City Hall."

Mr Lorenzo slammed his door, leaving me chuckling in the lobby. On my way upstairs, I stopped at the third-floor landing and stared at the door to 303. I considered knocking but continued up the stairs. Then, I heard pots and pans tumbling inside. I went back down and knocked. After another chorus of falling pots, the deadbolt clunked, and Mrs Cazares swung open the door. She scrutinized me, looking somewhat out of sorts. But then again, she always looked like that.

"Hi, Mrs Cazares. I just wanted to stop by and make sure you were okay."

"Why wouldn't I be? I've got too many damn pots in the cupboard, is all. You and Whitney need any pots or pans?"

"Whit's mom just bought us a new set," I smiled, knowing her kitchenware was probably ancient. "Actually, what I meant was...about last night."

"Why? What happened last night?"

"You screamed. Real loud. Must've been almost two o'clock. Didn't you?"

"If I did, I don't know about it. Didn't wake up. Slept like the—" She cut off abruptly and stared past me onto the landing. I turned around to see who was there, but there was no one. "Now that you mention it, I did have a nasty dream. Can that happen?"

"What?"

"You know...you scream in the dream and it comes out of your mouth for real. But without waking up?"

"Sure it can. People do all sorts of nutty things in their sleep. Sometimes, Whit gets up and brushes her teeth in the middle of the night without knowing she's doing it. One time, she told me she'd been dreaming about...uh, never mind..." I trailed off in embarrassment, but I'd already said too much.

"About what?" prodded Mrs Cazares.

"No, nothing."

"Don't be a tease, young man. Spit it out. I can handle it."

"She told me...she said she'd been dreaming about...eating human flesh."

"*Agghh!*" she winced.

"You asked!" I laughed.

"Never mind what I asked. Don't tell me things like that, kid. You're gonna give me more nightmares that way... Although, you saying that just reminded me what it was about."

"Your dream?"

With a grimace, she nodded. "My daughter."

"I didn't know you had a daughter."

Averting her eyes, Mrs Cazares sighed and spoke softly. "She left home before you and Whitney moved in. Been a long time since I've seen her. Or heard from her. We had a...difficult relationship. Never saw eye-to-eye on much of anything. And I wasn't a great mother. She came home. In the dream, she came home...to kill me."

"Jesus, that's, uh... I mean, can I do anything? To help or, I don't know..."

Mrs Cazares smiled and shook her head. "Was it that loud? My scream? Others heard it, too?"

I nodded, uncomfortable with the way she was staring at me, her eyes bulging out of her face. "I'm sure they did."

"That explains what Henny said to me."

"What'd he say?"

"Something about putting me out of my misery. Ornery old crank. Oughtta put himself out of his own misery. Do us all a favor."

"You sure you're alright, Mrs Cazares?"

"Nothing but a bad dream. Thanks, Nate. You know, you're the only one who came to ask about it. Sweet of you. Tell Whitney I said hi, okay?"

As I slipped my key into our door, Ben Grafton came out of 402. He lives there with his girlfriend, Dawn Ulmer. They're an opinionated couple who often sound like they're arguing, but really, they just get passionate no matter the topic. Ben and I chatted for a few minutes, his voice reverberating down the stairwell. He told me he'd heard the scream but fell right back to sleep, and so did Dawn. He wasn't surprised when I told him it was Mrs Cazares, but the details of her nightmare freaked him out. He asked me not to mention it to Dawn and then slunk back into their apartment.

That night, I was out cold before ten o'clock and probably having the best sleep since I was a baby.

Just after midnight, Mrs Cazares screamed again. It happened earlier than the night before but just as loud. Whit was in bed with me, still awake with a psychology textbook and making notes for her master's thesis. The scream brought me shooting up so violently that I disrupted the comforter, which knocked the book from Whit's hands. It crashed to the floor with a heavy thud. Instantly, the scream died off, like a hand had been clapped over the offending mouth.

Taking long, deep breaths, I stared at Whit. She looked back at me, stunned by both the scream and my reaction.

"*That's* what you heard last night?"

It took me a while to gather my thoughts. I nodded. "Mrs Cazares."

"I hope she's alright." She reached over the side of the bed for her book. "I'd bet this woke her up. Probably for the best. Poor lady."

Whit kept making notes for another hour or so. I cuddled up beside her. Rather than keeping me awake, the bedside lamp and the gentle scratching of Whit's pencil helped me fall back to sleep. An anxious, queasy sleep, but better than nothing.

My body felt more rested in the morning, but not my mind. It felt uneasy, distracted, thin.

That day passed much the same as the previous day. I got through work by using simple rationalizations to calm my mind in gradual increments. Now that I knew the reason for Mrs Cazares's screams, I worried less about her or what I could do. No more fantasies of break-ins or midnight prowlers. But my lack of control began to bother me. Why should I be so haunted by someone else's nightmares?

By the end of the workday, I felt better but not nearly as good as the day before. Coming into our building, I ran into Fred Moore, the ninety-one-year-old widower from 102. On nice days, he likes to sit on a lawn chair on the front stoop. Even with his hearing aids, Mr Moore can barely hear a thing.

I came up the steps and shouted, "Howdy, Freddy!" He appeared not to have heard me, so I waved my hand in a big, exaggerated arc, which he didn't seem to see. I wondered if he'd started to lose his eyesight, too, but when I passed beside him, he suddenly grabbed my wrist and pulled me close.

"Tell that woman on three to keep it down," he grumbled.

"You heard her scream?"

"What's that?"

"Never mind…"

On the second-floor landing, Sue Demarco and Noreen Spinks stood outside their apartments complaining about Mrs Cazares while Noreen's kids played on the stairs. Ironically, neither woman seemed to have a problem with the kids screaming up a storm.

On three, Henrick Lewiston had his door open. He was leaning against the doorframe, sucking on a bottle of Budweiser, and scowling across the landing at Mrs Cazares's door. I paused to stare at him, hoping that would send him back inside. But a hardheaded alcoholic like Henrick wasn't about to be intimidated by a scrawny desk jockey like me. The way he stared at her door—like he was one beer away from kicking it in—really bothered me. Mrs Lisotho once told me that Henrick had a history of violence. Used to spend several weeks a year in prison for bar fights, domestic battery, and destruction of property.

I wanted to say something, but I only showed my disapproval with a shake of the head before continuing up the stairs. I had a bad feeling that he would do something to Mrs Cazares. I didn't know what. Spook her or knock her around or something. But what could I do about it? More than anything, I just wanted the whole ordeal to go away.

No such luck. I struggled to fall asleep that night. Whit stayed up late, working on her thesis again, but she did it at the dining table. I tossed and turned for a few hours, drifting in and out of a porous veneer of sleep. When Whit came to bed, I felt paralytic with fatigue, but I still couldn't conk out. The longer this went on, the more anxious I became. My heart accelerated toward an inevitable explosion. Five minutes after Whit's head hit the pillow, I heard her breathing plateau into a steady rhythm. An irrational jealousy almost convinced me to grab her and shake her awake. The coughing from the alleyway started up again, with less frequency than a few days earlier but still persistent enough to drive me up the wall.

Finally, at half-past three, she screamed. Though I didn't shoot out of bed this time, I still became fully alert. My eyes shot open. I clutched at the comforter, my body stiff as a corpse. Then, in the silence that followed, a sense of relief washed over me, like slipping into a hot bath after being out in freezing temperatures all day.

I finally relaxed somewhat, allowing sleep to catch up. Just as I dropped off, I considered the sick logic of what had happened—the anticipation of Mrs Cazares's scream had kept me awake. As soon as I heard it, my mind and body started to shut down naturally. I slept the rest of the night without issue. Even though I got less than five hours, it was my first solid sleep in two days.

Contrary to my hopes, things didn't improve much. In fact, they got worse. Once I realized that my subconscious was sidelining sleep until it heard the expected scream, I spent every waking hour wondering what the night would bring. How long would I have to wait? And how would my mind deal with the stress of waiting?

I thought a lot about the nightmares that caused her screams, too. After talking to Mrs Cazares a few more times, I learned that her daughter, Julieta, continued to visit her dreams, always coming with the same purpose—to take her mother's life. Not once did Mrs Cazares wake up as a result of her screams. Instead, after the moment of attack, when most people would wake up in hysterics, she kept dreaming. She saw Julieta coming toward her with a weapon that changed from night to night. A blade, a hammer, her hands, a lethal dose of Fentanyl. Julieta would throw herself on top of her, hold her down on the mattress, and do the deed, at which point Mrs Cazares screamed. Or so she assumed. Since she didn't wake up, she couldn't know for sure whether the screams aligned with the events in her dreams. But in Mrs Cazares's own words, "After Julieta attacks me, I continue to dream…of death."

Mrs Cazares was either unwilling or unable to elaborate. This gnawed at me. What did it mean to dream of death? Simply considering the prospect sent chills down my spine. Even trying to imagine such a dream felt like having an army of fire ants loose inside my skull. I wanted to understand what she meant but also forget that I had even heard her say it.

Each night, the scream came at a different time. In general, it happened sometime between one and two o'clock. Once, it came early, before midnight. Another time, it came around four-thirty. I tried everything to knock myself out before the scream. Sleeping pills, earplugs, a blackout mask, weed, and soothing background music. I cut caffeine out of my diet. I tried sleeping in another room. Evening exercise, hot baths, sex, meditation. Nothing worked. Every night, I remained on edge, an uptight, nervous wreck right until the moment Mrs Cazares screamed.

After the fifth day, I checked on her every morning before work. At first, she seemed annoyed by my visits, but I soon learned it wasn't because of me. She said a few of the other tenants had been acting funny. Mrs Lisotho from next door avoided her. Henrick Lewiston threatened to come in and shut her up for good. Kevin Park from 401 told everyone in the building he might move out because of Mrs Cazares. Old Freddy Moore, sitting sentry in his lawn chair, chastised her every time she came or went, telling her she deserved to go nuts after what she did to her daughter. Mr Lorenzo gave her two written warnings, threatening to call the building owner and the cops. Noreen Spinks's kids would mimic the screams when they played in the stairwell. Even the homeless guy from the alley got caught up in it. Some nights, he'd cry. Other nights, he screamed himself. On Friday, he upset all the trash cans on the block, and on Saturday, he yelled, "Shut up! Shut up!" for twenty minutes straight. Then, on Sunday, a few people swore they heard him singing a lullaby. Others thought it might have been a hymn. Dawn and Ben found out his name was Stephen, so they started calling him Steve-o the Schizo.

Despite all the tenants talking about her, Mrs Cazares didn't blame them. Instead, she blamed herself for becoming the building nuisance. Feeling bad for her, Sue Demarco and Whitney tried to help by spending time with her. They accompanied her on errands, took her out to lunch, helped clean hard-to-reach spots in her apartment, that sort of thing. And even though I was dealing with my own nerves from lack of sleep, I continued to stop by every morning just to chat.

Then, I started to mess up at work. I had trouble showing up on time or focusing during the day. I fell asleep at my desk, forgot to complete assignments, and became irritable with coworkers. Though I only got a few hours of sleep each night, I started having nightmares of my own. Whit slept, but restlessly. She kicked and thrashed around, cracking me in the mouth with a closed fist on one occasion. I woke around quarter to three one night to find her half of the bed empty. The apartment was dark. When I called her name, I got no response, so I got up and found her in the bathroom, brushing her teeth in the dark. She was totally zoned out. Somehow, I got her to rinse her mouth and brought her back to bed, but there was no way I could fall back to sleep that night. Her eyes were closed—I checked—but I couldn't shake the feeling that she was watching me. Leering at me gluttonously. The next morning, she woke up crying but had no recollection of what happened.

At that point, I had to question my sanity. I'd been functioning on a few questionable hours of sleep per night for almost two weeks. As if Mrs Cazares's dreams hadn't wound me up enough, now I had my own nightmares to deal with. And my wife was dreaming about cannibalism again.

Mr Lorenzo finally called the cops on Steve-o the Schizo. When two officers showed up, Lorenzo used the opportunity to take them up to 303. Not happy about being taken advantage of, the officers spoke to Mrs Cazares for two minutes, then told Mr Lorenzo there was nothing they could do about it. They refused to do anything about the homeless guy either, stating that new regulations forbade them from forcibly removing "unhoused" folks unless they had committed a crime. Since Steve's effects were gathered near the basement entrance to the neighboring building, he wasn't trespassing on our property. The superintendent of that building hates Mr Lorenzo's guts. So, purely out of spite, he refused to file a complaint, meaning the cops had their hands tied. Before they left, they gave Mr Lorenzo a public reaming in the lobby, which drew everyone out of their apartments. Everyone except Mrs Cazares.

Whit suggested I stay up late and try to be productive. I decided to give it a shot, but I couldn't focus. I tried researching some night courses to advance my career, then gave up and worked on fixing the uneven legs on our coffee table. That led to rearranging the furniture. Since I was barely paying attention, the living room ended up looking like a storage garage. I put all the furniture back where it was, read for a bit, watched some reruns, and finally fell to staring out the window. The act of consciously trying to distract myself seemed to tilt my mind even further toward the eventual scream. I became a jittery mess as the night wore on, agitated by...by what? I didn't even know anymore. Was it the screams? The unrest in the building? Mrs Cazares's nightmares? Or Whit's? Or my own? Lack of sleep? The looming threat of madness?

Dead tired, I gave up around a quarter to four. The thought

of brushing my teeth gave rise to visions of Whitney feasting on my innards while I slept, so I skipped it. However, knowing it wouldn't be long before the scream came, I did feel a brief sense of peace when my head hit the pillow. Whit was asleep on her stomach. Every couple of minutes, her right leg rose up and kicked the mattress. I didn't hear anything from Steve-o the Schizo in the alley. The cough medicine must have helped.

Soon, just like every other night, the silence began to get to me. It reminded me of that first night. I closed my eyes and counted the days since the first scream. Thirteen. *Fuckin' A*, I thought, *of course it's thirteen.* I'd never been superstitious or anything, but I'd grown up with the tales of unlucky thirteen. Hard to ignore something like that when you're already halfway into a meltdown. My mind took that stupid, useless tidbit and ran with it, twisting it into an omen of excruciatingly immediate significance. Other imagined omens wandered into my thoughts. The chipped mirror in our bathroom. The black tomcat that stalked our block. The light in the stairwell that kept shorting out. How I lost my wedding band on our honeymoon. The fatal car accident that happened at a crosswalk—two feet from the tip of my nose—when I was eleven years old.

Whit was fast asleep, but she began to make this gross sound like she was gagging on something. She stopped every time I looked at her but then started again. Finally, I shook her by the shoulder until she cleared her throat and flopped onto her back.

The silence resumed. The clock on my phone became a lifeline. I checked it every ten minutes. The intervals decreased to five minutes, three, two. One. Time didn't stop, but my brain could no longer recognize its reliable flow. I stared at the numbers. They remained unchanged no matter how long I watched them. Then I'd blink, and they would have jumped ahead fifteen, twenty, forty-five minutes.

The silence drowned me. Shadows lurked in the living room and crawled through the darkness in the bedroom. My body ached with the tension of waiting. Screams echoed in my mind. They were not the mindless, deafening screams of mortal terror but only my own desperate wails begging for help. I realized that I wanted—no, I needed—Mrs Cazares to shatter the silence so I could get some sleep.

Five o'clock came and went.

Six o'clock.

The first light of dawn began to spill through the windows. Fear wrapped its cold hands around my ankles, slowly crawling up my legs, a corpse dragging itself out of the grave. With each passing minute, it reached further up my body until it lay splayed across me, crushing me with its frigid, reeking dead-weight, whispering into my ear, *She's not going to scream, she's not going to scream...*

If Mrs Cazares did not scream, I knew I would never be able to fall asleep.

As dawn crept on toward morning, I lay in bed with that weight rotting on top of me. All the awful visions and omens and crippling tension of another sleepless night remained, promising to stay with me throughout the day unless I heard the scream. The light of morning filtered into the apartment. The flesh of the stinking carcass lying on top of me decayed, but I knew it was still there. It broke apart and melted away, absorbed into my body, a permanent fear that would grow unchecked, like a landfill for lost hopes and dreams.

When I finally got up, without having slept a single minute, permanent fear had taken hold. Whit woke up and gaped at the sight of me, pale shock plastered on her face. She said something, but I didn't hear what. Pulses of living terror ripped through me, telling me to get back into bed and stay there, telling me to run and never look back, telling me to launch myself out the window onto the concrete four stories below.

"Why? Why would I do that? I just need some sleep..."

The fear answered me.

What will you do if she never screams again?

The thought of even one more night like that brought me to my knees.

"Nate?" Whit jumped out of bed. "Nathan, what? What is it?"

And I screamed. A high-pitched, terror-filled, hair-raising scream, loud and frenzied enough to rival any of Mrs Cazares's.

But it didn't matter. I could scream all I wanted. My screams would never help me sleep. They would only keep ratcheting up the fear until I heard the scream I needed to hear.

PICNIC WITH MOMMY AND HER FRIEND

They take the bus, riding past all the stops where they would normally get off. Several times, the boy asks where they're going, but Mommy ignores him. All the riders get off, and new riders take their places. The scenery out the windows gradually changes, the buildings shrinking away into the distance. When they've ridden all the way out of the city, Mommy finally answers, huffing with irritation that they're going on a picnic. The boy's eyes light up as he gazes at the fields and trees surrounding them, but then he stares at Mommy in confusion. They don't have a picnic basket. All Mommy brought along was a paper grocery bag, which he'd assumed was full of the usual junk she carried around. Now, he wonders if it contains the necessities for a picnic. He knows better than to ask any more questions, so he contents himself with the belief that it's just him and his mother, alone for an entire day. Maybe she will play with him in the grass or help him catch toads near a pond. They can take a nap together, snuggling close and finding shapes in the clouds. Share sandwiches, cookies, ice cream, and juice—if that's what the paper bag contains. Nothing can go wrong. Mommy won't get angry. She can't scream at him out here since there is nothing to upset her. Maybe she won't even hit him today. On such a beautiful day, how could she?

The farther they get from the city, the more confident he becomes that it's going to be a wonderful day.

After the bus lets them off on the side of the road, they follow a dirt path into a barren field. The grass rises above the boy's head. Walking fast, Mommy holds his hand, not so much out of affection as to drag him along.

She must be excited for the picnic, too, thinks the boy.

Seconds after hearing the water of the nearby creek, the boy sees the car parked at the end of the dirt path. A shit-brown Dodge Dart, the newest model, 1973—though the boy doesn't know or care what it is. It could be a bicycle with two flat tires or NASA's newest Apollo spacecraft, but when his mother drops his hand and runs toward the vehicle, her squeal of delight tells the boy all he needs to know—that big hunk of metal means this picnic is not for him and Mommy. It's there to ruin his day.

And it doesn't take long. The man standing by the hood makes sure of that. A cigarette dangles from his lips, his arms are tattooed with lewd pictures, and a dark stream of piss arcs away from his waist. He saunters toward them, still zipping his fly, and grabs the boy's mother by the waist, giving the boy a brief repellent glare before dragging Mommy through the tall grass.

By the time the boy catches up, they have already spread out a stained, holey blanket. The paper bag lies forgotten in the grass. The boy picks through it, finding nothing to his liking, so he goes off to play near the stream. Neither Mommy nor the man notices him leave.

After a while, he hears Mommy screaming like she sometimes does at home, not yelling at the boy in anger but screaming out to God.

Standing in the cool water, the boy glances back. Through the grass, he can see Mommy on all fours, like an animal, with the man mounting her from behind. Digging his hand into Mommy's hair, he tugs her head back so she's looking at the sky as she cries God's name. The boy knows God is supposed to be up there, though he has never seen Him.

The boy doesn't much like the look of that man, but there were always men coming around the apartment that he didn't like. And they never cared for him either. They always said things like, "The kid gets in the way. How'm I supposed to get it up when the goddamn brat's right here in the room with us?" And Mommy would say, "Nothin' he hasn't seen before, so come on, big boy. What are you waiting for? Stay more than an hour and it'll cost you." Then they would argue a bit more, and maybe the man would swing a fist at Mommy or the boy until Mommy finally relented and sent the boy outside to play on the stoop.

So, knowing it's what Mommy would want, the boy follows the stream as far away as he can get. He doesn't really want to go back to their filthy, tiny apartment anyhow. He doesn't want Mommy or those strange men to hit him or call him names anymore. He would much rather stay here where it's quiet and serene. It smells nicer here than it does at home. There's fresh air and clean water. He hasn't seen any animals yet, but they must be around. And just like in the cartoons, the animals might make better companions than Mommy or those men.

If he can't enjoy a picnic with Mommy, he'll find some cuddly critters to spend the day with instead. Maybe he'll even stay with them, like the boy in the jungle, Mowgli.

He follows the stream, splashing through the shallow water. When it gets deeper, he crosses to the other side and dashes through a line of trees. Soon, he emerges in another field, this one stretching as far as the eye can see. He keeps running until he no longer hears Mommy screaming to God, then stops to catch his breath and appreciate the silence.

But the silence disappears almost at once. He hears something nearby, almost like a child crying. It gets closer. Ahead of him on the vast plain, a patch of grass sways as something approaches. Now, it sounds more like laughter. A kid his own age, perhaps. Or a mischievous grandfather who lives all alone out here, tittering to himself about the pitfalls of growing old. The laughter contains no joy but becomes more manic and contemptuous as it draws near. The boy knows he should run. He should go back to Mommy and the strange man with the pictures on his arms, blowing smoke from his nostrils and scowling like the boy is some kind of vermin.

No, this is better. He belongs here, out in the grass with the laughter and—

"*Oof!* Hey—"

The blow to the boy's stomach has knocked the wind out of him. He's on his back, gasping and blinking away tears. As he stares upward, he notices the cloud directly overhead. It looks just like one of the Seven Dwarfs. He can't decide which one. Maybe Doc. Or Dopey.

When the boy finally gets up, he sees the bully who knocked him over.

A goat.

The animal's white coat is soiled and matted with dried mud, twigs, and dead insects. As the boy lifts himself to his feet, the goat grinds its front hooves into the grass, lowering its head to show off its two massive horns and threatening to charge again. A long clump of dark fur hangs from its chin. Grunting, it stares at the boy and seems to relax when it observes his slight stature, no taller than the goat itself.

Gradually, the boy catches his breath. He continues rubbing his ribs where the goat rammed him, and he glares at the animal mistrustfully, like he wants revenge. But, in truth, he would prefer to make friends.

The goat begins to pace, keeping at a slight distance from the boy but not retreating. It snorts repeatedly in a curious way that resembles the men who come around to see Mommy. They often walked around the apartment, naked and cursing, just like this goat. As the goat walks back and forth, its eyes remain fixed on the boy.

From behind, a frantic scream rings out, carrying over the stream and the field, this one even louder and more passionate than Mommy's other screams.

The goat stops pacing and abruptly stands on its hind legs, towering over the boy as it squints into the distance. Then, it laughs again as it tilts its head down at the boy.

Staring at the animal in shock, the boy remembers the goats at the zoo. When the children held out handfuls of pellets to feed them, they would bleat chaotically. But the goats at the zoo sounded nothing like this. What the boy hears now does not resemble laughter—it *is* laughter.

And those goats never stood on two legs.

Suddenly, the creature makes a new sound. The boy spins around, thinking at first that Mommy's friend has come to fetch him. But no...

That was the goat, too.

Staring up and stumbling backward, the boy gapes at the animal, still standing tall on two legs. It lets out a short bleat before repeating the unbelievable sound.

"They have forsaken you," it says in a low, sneering voice.

"Did you... D-d-did you just s-speak?"

"Are you a halfwit? Is that why they forsake you?" The goat laughs again. This time, it sounds like the villain on a late-night TV program.

"I don't know what that means," answers the boy.

Dropping down onto four legs, the goat trots forward. It

lowers its head threateningly, showing its horns but only giving the boy a playful nudge. As it rubs its coarse fur against the boy's body, it coerces him to run his hands through its coat. After a few minutes of this petting, it jams its snout into the boy's forehead.

"It means your mother dislikes you. You grew from spoiled seed, and she seeks to rid herself of that burden. Even now, she is collecting fresh seed for a new bastard to replace you." The goat grins and licks its lips. "She never loved you."

"No..."

"Do you love your mother, boy?"

"I do. I love her, but..."

"But she ignores you, doesn't she? She welcomes the stench and filth of other men, filling herself with them, reserving only the back of her hand for you. She curses you every day. What does she call you, I wonder? Her mistake? Little bastard? Bane of her existence?"

"She calls me..." The boy shakes his head and looks at the ground. Sniffling, he takes a deep breath. "She calls me...'My fucking curse.'"

The goat's bleating rises into a more malevolent laughter. A thick cloud covers the sun, casting a shadow over the field. Mottles appear on the goat's coat, and the boy cannot recall whether they were there before.

"Clever," wheezes the goat as its laughter winds down. "Would you like to earn her attention? Do you desire mother's love?"

The mere thought of it nearly brings the boy to tears. Not wanting to weep in front of this animal, he takes several more deep breaths to steady his nerves and nods, *Yes, yes, Mommy's love is all I've ever wanted.*

"I can help you. Will you do as I say?" the goat asks, rising onto its hind legs again.

"Who are you?"

"Today, I am your friend. Tomorrow, I am you. We can be together forever, just like you wished. I heard your prayer. But the world is larger than you think. It contains the potential for boundless happiness, but you must be hardy of body and mind. I can show you how. Wouldn't you like that? To be my friend for all time? Just do as I say, and we can be together. You and Mommy and m-meh-eh-eh!"

It bleats this last word, a sinister utterance that once more makes the boy consider running back toward the stream, shouting for Mommy to save him from this unnatural beast. However, when he glances back at the tall grass, more clouds roll in, rendering the world even gloomier and reminding the boy why he ran into the field in the first place—*because Mommy does not want me.*

"Do you know why she brought you here?" asks the goat, responding to the boy's private thoughts. "She could have let that prick fuck her anywhere. But out here, in the middle of nowhere, she hoped you would run away and get lost, just as you have done. She prayed for this. Prayed to be rid of you."

"How do you know that?"

The goat snorts. "But it's not right, is it? I've come to steer you back toward the light, little one. To give your mother the fright she deserves. It's simple, what I ask of you. Don't worry. It's just a simple thing, but it will earn you her respect."

"Will she love me?"

"She will have to. If she doesn't, I'll show you what to do."

Tears roll down the boy's cheeks, tears of joy at the thought of having Mommy's love. He blinks to clear his eyes and imagines himself sleeping in bed with Mommy, cradled in her arms without the scowling men who shout at him and chase him out. He wants to feel Mommy's arms wrapped around him, not them. He wants to bury his face in her breast and breathe in her musk untainted by the smell of those men. Mommy should belong to him and no one else.

The boy looks at the goat and nods. "Okay."

"That's a good boy," it bleats and laughs. "The rewards for brave little boys like you last a lifetime. You will discover true bliss and pleasure. But your end will be painful."

"What does that mean?"

"Someday you will know. Do not worry, child. It will only be what you deserve and nothing more. Now, follow me."

Walking on its hind legs, the goat disappears into the grass. The boy hesitates. He had not expected the creature to lead him farther away. He thought it would take him back to Mommy. With a glance back, the boy wonders one last time if he should run. Maybe he doesn't even have to return to Mommy and the man. He can keep following the stream away from them and the goat. There must be somebody who will love him.

"F-follow you where?" the boy says, hardly loud enough for the goat to hear.

"It is nearby," bleats the goat, its voice already fading. "Come to me. I won't ask much, and it won't hurt."

"It won't?" The boy steps toward the voice, not because he wants to go to the goat but simply because he doesn't want to feel alone anymore.

"No, it won't hurt you. Not yet. Keep coming. You're almost here. Just a little farther..."

The boy emerges into a narrow clearing, maybe five feet wide and ten deep. The goat is on all fours again. As it gazes at him, the boy notices the brilliant blue shade of its eyes. He hadn't noticed them before. In fact, he thought they'd been reddish. Bleating dumbly, the goat nods down at the grass between them. A broken wine bottle lays on its side on a round spot of flattened grass, almost like a platter. The base has been shattered away, leaving a jagged circle of jutting spikes.

Again, the goat bleats. It turns to the side, showing the boy its white flank. Strangely, its fur is no longer filthy or mottled.

It's pure white—flowing, silky, and angelic. The dark clouds have moved on, leaving the sunlight to splash the boy's cheeks. In the light, the goat's fur looks like unsullied cotton, a plush doll, or an inviting pillow. Now, more than ever, the boy wishes to touch it. He wants to keep the goat as a pet and run his hands through its fur forever. To fall asleep with his arms wrapped around its neck. He doesn't need to go back with Mommy. He can live here with the goat. It can look after him, teach him, love him.

A sharp grunt erupts from the goat. It sounds like a particular swear word that the men sometimes growl at the boy. The goat gives another short bleat, glances at the bottle, and then trots away.

"No!" shouts the boy as he lunges forward.

Startled by the sound, the goat stops and looks around. When it sees the boy coming at him, it's too late for either of them to retreat. The boy has already picked up the broken bottle and sprung at the animal, slashing at its hind leg. The glass opens a deep wound, spraying blood all over the boy and rendering the leg useless. The goat's hindquarters droop to the ground, but it struggles on, frantically prancing with its forelegs, bleating and whining as it tries to pull itself away. Before it gets too far, the boy stabs it in the flank. The bottle's two dozen razor points sink into the goat's flesh. A few of them snap off between the ribs. The goat tumbles onto its side, its bleating reduced to a hoarse, panicked wheezing.

When the boy pulls out the bottle, blood spurts and flows from the wound. An oozing, crimson waterway rapidly drenches the snow-white coat. The boy continues stabbing, thrashing, and slashing until the bottle has fractured into several unmanageable fragments. After that, the boy continues pummeling the lifeless animal with his hands, driven by a ravenous urgency he has never known before. There's a warm tingle in his chest and a curious sense of recognition that tells him he's doing the right thing—the only thing. He finally pulls himself off the animal when he can no longer lift his arms.

For maybe five minutes, the boy lies in the sopping grass beside the dead goat. They're lying in a puddle of blood, but the boy hardly notices. He's beginning to feel something else and trying to remember what the goat called it—

Bliss and pleasure.

Before the boy leaves, he uses what's left of the bottleneck to carve off a section of the goat's hide. On his way back to the picnic site, he wades across the stream again. This time, he pauses in the middle and washes the blood off the scrap of goat flesh, hoping to return the fur to the pure white he'd seen just before it was stained. He scrubs, watching the red trails swept away in the current.

The white fur is still slightly pink, but it's as clean as he can get it. As he approaches, the boy can see Mommy and the man lying naked on the picnic blanket. They are both smoking, and neither seems to have heard him coming. He steps out of the stream, slipping on the bank. The water has washed the blood from his legs and feet, but he hasn't bothered to splash water over the rest of his body. His face, arms, and chest are still slathered in gore.

"Mommy!" he calls out. The man leans up and gazes around. "Mommy! I got something for you!"

"The fuck is that?" shouts the man, leaping off the blanket. He searches for his clothes but keeps looking down at the boy. "That your fuckin' brat?"

Mommy screams, covering her breasts as she scrambles away on her backside.

The boy holds out the scrap of flesh, roughly the size of a slice of bread.

"It's for you, Mommy..."

The man squints at it, then relaxes his tense shoulders. Chuckling, he steps toward the boy.

"Hank!" shrieks Mommy. "What have you done, Hank? You perverted little fuck! You're a curse on my life! What did you do, you creep?"

Suddenly, Mommy stops crawling backward. She crouches, snarls, and flings herself at the boy, her hands outstretched.

As she flies at him, the man winds up and lays a backhand into Mommy's face. Her nose explodes. Blood pours down her lips and chin. She curls into a ball on the blanket, groaning in pain.

"You fuck! You motherfucker! You broke my nose, you—"

"Shut up, bitch," says the man. "The kid brought you a present. Looks like a fine present, too. This is one helluva boy you got here. Ain't gonna let you smack around a good, strong-minded boy like this."

Hank stares at the man in awe. No one has ever said such kind things about him before.

"That's a damn nice piece of flesh you got there, boy. Hank, was it?"

The boy nods, his eyes bright and wide as he stares at the man. He holds the scrap of flesh out, offering it to the man rather than his mother.

With a wide, toothy grin, the man takes it. "Look at that—hell yeah! You's a good boy, young Hank Tinkerman. Gonna make somethin' of yerself, I can feel it. Gonna be a *real man*. And your mother better be proud of you, or she's gonna have trouble coming her way. Ain't that right, Hank?"

The man starts to laugh, and when the boy realizes his laughter sounds exactly like the goat's, he joins in, laughing harder than ever before.

A FOG TOO DENSE

Last night, I crossed the river by foot without bridge or boat. I'm not trying to tell a riddle or anything; there's just no other way to say it. I missed work today. Didn't even call in to let them know. And I've been sitting here by the window all day, staring at a familiar scene that no longer feels so familiar.

At one kilometer across, the Han River is no skinny blood vessel but a bulbous artery winding through the center of Seoul. Flying overhead at night, you can see it cutting a dark gash through the brilliant city lights, bridges laid across like the rungs of a ladder with freeways slithering along either side.

Seoul is one of those cities that never truly sleeps. Anywhere you go, you'll find twenty-four-hour convenience stores, restaurants and bars open until dawn. The hum of electricity is in the air, vibrations in the ground. Streetlights provide a palliative orange glow, and the signage in some areas glows brighter than daylight. There are, of course, back alleys that remain unlit and creepy. Certain neighborhoods hide shadowy corners and nooks, decrepit old structures, and winding dead-end streets that leave you stranded on the edge of nowhere.

I'm not Korean, but I've lived in Seoul long enough to consider it home. Fall is by far the best season. The monsoon rains and the humidity depart suddenly at the end of summer, but the temperatures remain pleasant and warm, with crisp, gentle breezes day and night. And there's a lightness, a freshness to the air, too, because it's the only time of year unaffected by the yellow dust that rolls in from the Gobi Desert. During the day, the sky is a vivid, dreamy blue with spots of fat, fluffy cloud cover that you wish you could sink your hands into. Crisp visibility allows you to stand on the modest hills south of the Han River and see clear across the city to the mountains of Bukhan National Park at the northern edge. The sky opens wide at night, revealing the few stars bright enough to penetrate the light pollution.

Yesterday was one of those days. I came home just before seven o'clock after an uneventful day at work. I was lagging, a bit drawn out, but the view across the river always invigorates me on clear days like that. Our apartment is on the Han's north side, and directly across, nestled against the southern bank, lies the island of Yeouido. A narrow sliver of river branches off around this bit of land before rounding back to reunite with the main waterway. It's been built up over the years and now displays one of Seoul's finest skylines, a blend of towering financial powerhouses, corporate headquarters, and apartment complexes. The island also houses the National Assembly Building and the Yeouido Full Gospel Church, the country's largest house of Christian worship. Farther south, the peak of Mount Gwanak rises as a backdrop to that skyline, capped by radio and cell phone towers. The sharp, bright angles of the skyscrapers stand out like a postcard against the lush green slopes before the autumn colors take over. That picturesque view always used to be one of the best things about living near the river.

I stepped out to pick up some pork belly, garlic, and a few

beers for dinner. I noticed a chill in the air that hadn't been there when I got home half an hour earlier. A brisk breeze rolled in from the west. By the time I returned with the groceries, the breeze seemed to be dragging in a fog. A mist had rolled over the river, obscuring the building tops slightly and adding mystique to the evening view.

My wife came home from the gym as I was preparing dinner. She took a quick shower while I set out the food. As we ate, I tried to chat about work and make plans for the coming winter, but she didn't seem interested. She's been a bit distant ever since an argument we had a few weeks back. She accused me of something outrageous. Something I absolutely did not do. I don't have the faintest clue what gave her the idea in the first place, but it got so bad that she actually left town to visit her aunt for a few days. Then, while she was there, some sort of accident occurred and her aunt unexpectedly passed away. Naturally, it gave my wife quite a shock, and she came back in an even worse state than when she left. Suffice it to say, I still haven't managed to patch things up. Instead of pressuring her into light conversation, I turned my attention to my dinner while allowing my eyes to wander out the window.

The fog had grown thicker. The lights from the skyscrapers across the river had become faint orbs, diluted through the low gray clouds. The top floors of the tallest buildings were completely obscured. My wife asked what I was looking at.

"You're thinking about her again, aren't you?"

"This fog sure came on suddenly..." I replied, hardly hearing her.

"Hmph," she grunted and got up. When she set her dishes in the sink, she winced and grabbed her right shoulder. She told me she hurt it helping her aunt wrangle livestock a few days earlier. I know her aunt has a lot of animals, but that explanation seemed unlikely. Yu-mi isn't really the type to get her hands dirty. Rubbing her shoulder, she stomped past me and slammed the door to our bedroom. I heard it lock—my sign to sleep on the sofa again.

As I washed the dishes, I kept glancing out the window to watch the fog's progress. By the time I finished, I could only make out the faintest outlines of the buildings across the river. The headlights and taillights of cars crossing the Seogang Bridge seemed oddly diluted. City fog tends to collect and trap urban light, so the fog itself glows from inside. But the glow around Yeouido had never been so weak.

To take my mind off it, I busied myself with a few things around the house, shaking my head and mumbling about the fog's curious thickness. I called through the bedroom door to tell Yu-mi.

"It's only fog," she called back and refused to say more.

So, I cracked a beer and went onto the rooftop.

At first, I didn't trust what I was seeing. I put down my beer and rubbed my eyes. Fog blanketed the buildings on our side of the river, but beyond that it had gone pitch black. It looked like a dark curtain had been drawn across the sky. The street lights on the bridge shone spectrally through the fog and disappeared halfway across. I could no longer see any trace of the lights from Yeouido, only a flat, featureless darkness from a place where the lights should have been brightest. I figured there had to have been a power outage, but caused by what? Other than the fog, the weather was perfectly still. The mist brought on a chill, though there was almost no wind, which begged the question—How had the fog drifted in so quickly? And from where?

The more I stared at this blackness across the river, the more it sucked me in. At every moment, I expected my eyes to adjust and catch a glimmer peeking through, but I could not make out the slightest trace of light. Never a momentary inconsistency or a flicker. No sign of movement. Even the sounds of the city seemed dampened.

After almost two hours and four beers into my vigil, nothing had changed. My mind spun in search of an explanation, wired with the energy of trying to solve a mystery. No explanation I came up with made sense. I'd seen dense fog before, but never like this. I had to know. If I didn't get some sort of answer, it would bother me all night long.

I went back inside to grab a jacket. Not wanting to wake my wife, I left as silently as possible.

The fog had settled in the streets, too, but it was nowhere near as thick as across the river. I could still see the headlights of approaching cars, flashing crosswalk signs, and the sidewalk beneath my feet. I crossed under the westbound freeway through the damp pedestrian tunnel leading to the riverside. Old, yellow lights flickered and buzzed high on the walls. My anxious footsteps echoed in isolation.

From the riverside bike path, I should have had an unobstructed view of Yeouido. I assumed that reducing the distance would allow me to see into the fog and catch a glimpse of the structures I knew to be there. Instead, I stood dumbfounded— an idiot staring into a television screen that's not even switched on.

After a while, I noticed two things. When I looked up or downriver, the buildings and lights on the opposite bank were still visible. The dead shadow only shrouded the section of river directly across from me. Also, the darkness no longer looked like a curtain pulled across the river. It contained a peculiar sense of depth, as though you could reach into it. Sink or swim in it. Live in it.

That thought alone very nearly sent me high-tailing it back home. But there was also something terribly vexing about it; intoxicating, like the smell of a bonfire; inviting, like smoke from a chimney on a freezing night; provocative, like a neighborhood building set ablaze.

I stood against the railing. Below me, fog floated above the water. When I looked ahead, the water and mist both disappeared into that black gloom. Swallowed—that was how I thought of it at the time. To the east, the same thing happened to the Seogang Bridge. The bridge extended from my side of the river, lined with the haunting glow of streetlamps and flashing red suicide prevention lights. However, they ended halfway across as though the bridge had been abandoned in a state of half-completion. To the west, the same thing happened to the bridge for the trains of Line Two.

I'm not sure how long I stood there staring. I don't have any recollection of what was going through my head at that point or what happened next. Maybe I saw something and stretched for a better look, or I could have simply extended my upper body over the railing in a vain attempt to get closer. Either way, the next thing I knew, I was screaming and tumbling over the handrail. I heard a splash and felt the water soak my clothes. Flailing and spluttering, I managed to stand up. I didn't even realize that I wasn't sinking. I just looked around, stunned, confused, and wet.

The Han does not have a gradual drop. It's deep right up to the banks, so I should have sunk at once. But I didn't. I must have forgotten and assumed the water was shallow near the shore. Probably, my mind was too consumed with the fog to have considered it.

I stood up, patted myself down to check for injuries, and began searching for a way to climb back up. The fog made it difficult to see, and I took cautious steps to avoid a sudden drop-off.

As I walked, I squinted, peering into the haze under the belief that I was hugging the northern bank. When I reached out, however, my hands found no sign of the flood wall. Spinning around, I realized I had walked directly out into the river. Then, it finally occurred to me that I wasn't sinking. I wasn't floating either—certainly not walking on water or anything like that—but how else can I describe it? With each step, my foot plunged into the water slower than it should have, like stepping in fine sand, except my feet moved as smoothly as through a shallow puddle. Underneath the surface, my soles met resistance, holding me up. Though the water rarely rose above my ankles, I felt no solid surface beneath my feet. I couldn't—and still can't—imagine what my weight rested on or what my toes pushed off as I crept further into the fog-covered Han River.

Maybe ten meters out, I felt this extreme sense of shelter and peace. At that point, the fog was still visible, a veil of soft gray drifting past me. Holding my breath, I spun around on clumsy feet that were floating-not-floating, trying to appreciate the strange sensation of being suspended above the water. Ahead, a yawning opaque shroud still stretched over the island of Yeouido, rendering it absent from sight.

When I turned to the north to stare back at my side of the river, I thought about my wife sleeping in our apartment. I could almost feel the warmth of our bed and her body, both of which she had been denying me for weeks. The argument was about an ex-girlfriend of mine, someone I hadn't seen in at least ten years. Of course, I knew it was selfish to think my wife's foul mood had to do exclusively with me when her aunt had just passed away, apparently under pretty grisly and mysterious circumstances.

The intelligent thing to do would have been to go back home, get some rest, and try to talk to her in the morning. Hell, I probably should have been doing that the past few weeks. But she needed her space, and maybe I needed mine. What else was I doing standing in the river in the dead of night? How could I be so fascinated by a dense fog? Was it a trick of perception? A quirk of the light? Had I unwittingly shouldered some of my wife's stress, putting a strain on my mind?

These thoughts filled my head as long as I kept my back

turned on that predatory darkness. Thinking back, that would have been the moment to put my faith in sensible doubts and stop following the Pied Piper.

But I was already nearing the river's halfway point, still inexplicably floating, and I had to know why Yeouido had vanished.

That's when I heard a splashing sound off to my left. I thought about ducking under the water, but I didn't know how since I still wasn't sinking.

Then, I heard a voice. It sounded almost animal at first, a moaning wail borne of fright and exhilaration. I imagined someone losing their mind while in the throes of ecstasy. A form moved in the fog, wading-floating atop the river like me but farther to the east, near the Seogang Bridge. Though I couldn't see the trees, I realized the person was next to Bam Island, a small protected islet reserved for the use of migratory birds. They were standing on the silty western edge where the egrets congregate. When he spotted me, he stopped abruptly and began waving and shouting.

Becoming more used to how my feet settled in the water, I walked toward the islet, beckoning him toward me.

"Come out here! You won't believe this!" I called out in Korean. My voice sounded flat and labored in the fog. I waited until he got closer, then asked, "Do you have any idea what's going on?"

He came to within a meter of me before we could make out each other's features. He was about my age, wearing a cheap suit and dress shirt with his tie stuffed into his jacket's hip pocket. He looked startled when he saw me, likely not expecting to encounter anyone in the middle of the river, especially not a foreigner. Looking around apprehensively, he lifted one foot out of the water, gaping down in astonishment. "What is this?"

"I don't know," I said. "I don't understand why nobody else is out here. Doesn't anyone see it?"

"It's the middle of the night," he said as though it was obvious. "What are you doing out here?"

I shrugged. "I fell in…"

"How is it possible? To walk on the water? Like Jesus…"

"What about that?" I pointed at the gaping blackness across the river.

"What?" His eyes followed my hand, and he gasped. "What the…? Where's Yeouido?"

"That's why I came out here. I saw it from my apartment." I waited, assuming he would do something, like run back to the shore or take out his smartphone. But he only stared at the enormous wall of darkness ahead. I cleared my throat. "Do you want to check it out with me?"

He seemed uncertain as he tried to process what was happening, same as I had been doing for the past few hours. He put his hand on my shoulder and nodded without looking at me. "Are you sure it's safe?"

"No…but I can't stop thinking about it. It's burrowed into my mind."

He looked at me, confused by my wording. It's hard to get metaphorical speech right in your non-native language.

"Like a parasite," I said, referencing the Bong Joon-ho movie.

He exhaled with immediate understanding and nodded. "Okay."

We continued toward the invisible southern bank, moving slowly so he could get used to walking over the water. He told me his name was Sang-ho. He had been out drinking after work and knew he'd had too much, so he decided to walk off some of the alcohol. When he came out of the pub and saw the fog, it made him feel free somehow, like maybe he didn't have to go home or give his hard-earned money to his family anymore. This transitioned into a rant about how broke he was, complaining that most of his salary went to his parents. He had no recollection of how he got onto Bam Island.

Sang-ho's speech was slurred. He became more animated with every step, which made me uneasy. I know all too well that the unpredictable energy of a drunk can turn bitter and spiteful in an instant.

Just over halfway across the river, the blackness loomed overhead. It seemed to reach over us, like an overhanging cliff face, blending into the fog as though they originated from the same substance. Yet the yawning darkness bore no resemblance to clouds or mist. Unsteady on his feet, Sang-ho stared straight up, trying to see the top of it. He started to move faster, as if he had no intention of waiting for me anymore. Off to my right, I noticed a tiny shadow on the edge of the immense void.

I called out to Sang-ho. He looked back at me with uncontrolled agitation, on the verge of hysteria. I almost told him to go on alone. Instead, I gestured toward the figure on our right. Thinking it might be another person, I veered away from Sang-ho. After a moment, I heard his feet splashing after me.

Though I couldn't tell until I was right beside her, the motionless figure was a teenage girl. She was staring into the darkness ahead and didn't seem to have heard us. I said hello, but she didn't respond. More bluntly, Sang-ho yelled, *"Ya, michin sekki-ya!"* which roughly means, "Hey, you crazy bitch!" Still nothing. She stood and stared, transfixed by the towering emptiness.

I reached out to touch her shoulder. She jumped, gasping and gaping at me, her eyes stricken and hollow.

"Do you see anything?" I asked.

She stepped back, observing me carefully, then gazed at Sang-ho bobbing up and down, talking to himself as he inched forward.

"It's okay," I said. "I met him out here, just like you."

She glanced at the darkness again, then at me. We were all scared, but she looked more frightened than Sang-ho or myself and didn't bother to hide it.

Still, none of us had run off yet. We may have been scared, but we were also curious. Fascinated.

"Why did you come out here?" I asked.

She stared at me and noticed me looking at her pajama pants. "I was out...walking. On the bridge."

"The bridge?"

She nodded, gazing past me to where the southern portion of the Seogang Bridge should have been.

"You came down off the bridge?"

She stared at me again. "Yeah. I came down. And then I saw this. What about you?"

"I saw it from my apartment," I answered, gesturing toward the north shore.

"And?"

"I came out to get a closer look. Then, I...I fell in."

"And him?"

"I got lost," snapped Sang-ho.

"Yeah, well, I jumped."

"Jumped?" I repeated. It took a moment before I figured out what she meant. In a country with one of the highest suicide rates in the world, the bridges crossing the Han River serve as popular launching points.

She stared at me until the dawning light of understanding flashed in my eyes, then turned back toward the blackness.

"Oh..." I said. "Are you—"

"What is it?" the girl said before I could finish.

"I don't know."

"It's a black hole," said Sang-ho.

"I thought it was the fog," she answered. "But there's nothing there. Nothing at all. It's a...an absence."

"That's what I thought, too," I said. "And how are we walking in the river?"

She looked down at her feet, then at mine and Sang-ho's. Shrugging, she turned away and said, "What should we do?"

"We can't just stand here," I said.

"Why not? We already are."

"Because..."

"Maybe it's like a...a...what do you call it?" Sang-ho slurred. "A portal. Let's go inside."

The girl and I looked at each other.

"I'm Rick," I said. "And this is Sang-ho."

She smirked and nodded. "Mi-gyeong."

"Come on," said Sang-ho. He was bouncing and bobbing again, still stumbling on wobbly feet. "We've never seen anything like this. No one has. How can we pass it up? Huh? What luck... Three of us now... That's a lucky number! It's providence. It's destiny."

"It is kind of beautiful..." said Mi-gyeong.

"This is the craziest thing I've ever seen," I said. "What will happen to us if we go farther?"

"Discover another dimension," pleaded Sang-ho. "Like a multiverse. Didn't you see *No Way Home*? Three Spider-men, three of us. A real adventure to..." He trailed off into mumbled nonsense.

We all gazed forward, silent as we admired the confounding sight. It was not darkness like a room with no light, but rather total emptiness. No fog, no water, no shore, no buildings. And we stood right on the edge of it. Mi-gyeong had described it best—"*an absence.*"

I experienced a moment of profound apprehension and indecision. It felt as if I was looking upon a great discovery but privy to the knowledge that it would destroy the world if I let it out.

As I weighed the pros and cons, Mi-gyeong muttered, "What about the people?"

"What people?" I said, barely at a whisper.

"The people who li—"

"Screw the people, what about us?" blurted Sang-ho. "This is our chance."

"Chance for what?" I looked at him, but he had stepped ahead, so I could no longer see his face.

"To do something...special," he said. "Something different. To really do something that people will...respect."

"Why don't you go by yourself then?" spat Mi-gyeong.

"Maybe I will..." answered Sang-ho. But he didn't. He just stood there with us, gaping into what was not there.

Finally, I said, "I have to know."

Somehow, I knew I was saying what we were all thinking.

"Me, too," said Mi-gyeong.

And Sang-ho, "Okay."

We stepped forward, taking only a few steps before we were submerged in shadow. We still heard the water splashing around our feet and felt it soaking through our shoes and pants, but we could no longer see it. We walked directly beside one another, yet the others began to fade from sight. Mi-gyeong held her arms out in front of her, grasping for something, anything. I held out mine, too, though I didn't know what I thought I would find. I could barely see my hands at the end of my arms.

We walked like that for what seemed like a long time. If Yeouido was there, we definitely should have come upon its shore. There was nothing in front of us or around us. Only we three, somehow moving through that emptiness. I glanced over my shoulder and saw the north side of the river covered in a fog that glowed with the city lights, as fog usually looks. I could even pick out my apartment building. My wife and my life were back there. What the hell was I doing in this abyss?

Mi-gyeong gasped. I felt it, too—the water was gone. We still moved forward, but nothing lay beneath us. A wild sense of vertigo and dizziness rushed over me. Mi-gyeong grabbed my arm. I thought she did it to steady me, but then I realized she needed stability as much as I did. We held each other tighter, leaning into each other awkwardly, as strangers do. Soon, our hands were clasped together, more like lovers than strangers. Even so, we could barely see each other. And neither of us could see Sang-ho anymore.

I called out to him and got no response.

"Do you think we should go back?" said Mi-gyeong, trembling.

"We have to get Sang-ho."

"He creeped me out."

"Me, too. But we can't just leave him…"

I called out again. My voice sounded flat, without resonance or force, like something had sucked it right out of my mouth. This time, however, Sang-ho answered. His voice was more of a reverberation than a sound, the impenetrable darkness pulsing around us.

"Over here…hurry…"

"Where are you?" I screamed. Mi-gyeong joined me in calling out to him. We stuck close together, frightened and squeezing hands for added reassurance. We spun this way and that, even though all directions were the same—a colorless, featureless nothingness.

"Come on…this way…this is the way…" Sang-ho's voice came to us in rapid, garbled speech. He was using words I'd never heard before.

"Do you know what he's saying?" I asked Mi-gyeong. I had to pull her close and speak directly into her ear to be heard.

"Something about a new life. Or a pure life. Cleansing? The future? I don't understand. He sounds like a lunatic."

"Is that what this is?"

"What?"

"Are we losing our minds?"

"I already did... But now, I feel like I found something..."

"Yes...found something..." Sang-ho's voice came like a whisper whipping around us. "Found...something..." He broke off into manic laughter.

"He's drunk," said Mi-gyeong.

"I know, but we can't just let him..."

"Let him what? Die? Why not? Maybe he wants to die. I did."

"You don't anymore?"

"It feels like something is coming into my body. Coming in out of the darkness. It's dismantling me piece by piece...but not in a bad way. Like it will put me together again. Make me better. Brand new. Don't you feel it?"

"Yes..." I sighed. I didn't want to admit it, but I felt it, too. It felt like an orgasm sustained for minutes, hours on end. Even though I could no longer see her, I pulled Mi-gyeong closer. "I feel it. But we can't stay here. I don't think we're meant to."

"I know," she replied, slumping into my embrace.

"Let's try to find him, then we'll go back."

To be honest, I didn't really care what happened to Sang-ho. I hadn't felt it was my responsibility to find him until Mi-gyeong mentioned death. When she did, death seemed like the only real possibility left to us. It was present and immediate. We had waded into death's whirlpool willingly. If I hadn't beckoned to Sang-ho, he might have fallen into a peaceful drunken slumber on Bam Island instead of getting lost in this immersive void with me.

Suddenly, I felt both responsible for Sang-ho and incredibly protective of Mi-gyeong. I let go of her and gently pushed her toward the faint, distant lights on the north side of the river. Why did it seem so far away? It seemed unreachable, but I told her to go back.

"I don't want to go. Not alone. I'm scared..." she said, though she didn't sound scared. More like stoned.

"Get back to the shore," I said. "Far away from this. And stay away from the bridge."

She released an offended huff of air and muttered, "Fuck you."

I turned away from her and plunged into the blackness. It's hard to describe how I moved. It felt like swimming through sludge while simultaneously being swept along by a strong current. After a while, I glanced back and saw the lights of the northern shore fade away. I had an incomprehensible sensation of stasis and rapid movement happening at the same time. Voices seemed to inhabit the darkness, thousands of voices spitting and spinning in all directions. None of them sounded like Sang-ho's. I called out to him again but without conviction. By that point, I had already lost hope. I felt sure that he was gone for good and that I was next.

My efforts weened down to nothing. I let the strange current take me wherever it would, wondering how I was still breathing in this place. Shutting my eyes, I tried to drift off, hoping that I would go peacefully before being torn apart or crushed or ejected into space.

Suddenly, I ran into something. A body. Gasping for breath, I opened my eyes and realized it was Sang-ho. We were still inside the void, but I saw colors. I felt air. We were emerging from it.

The collision had sent Sang-ho drifting away from me and out of reach while I remained hovering in place. It looked like he had vomited on himself and then passed out. His head lolled back and forth as his body sank toward the ground.

The ground—catching sight of something recognizable quickly brought me back to my senses. I twisted around, trying to ascertain where we were, and realized we were floating about thirty meters above an unfamiliar and desolate country road.

Endless fields of grass stretched away on both sides. Though Sang-ho was moving downward, he was not plummeting but floating like a feather. A pair of headlights appeared, heading straight for him. I started to struggle, desperately squirming and wriggling to launch my body through the air, but I just hung there without resistance or anything to push off of.

All I could do was shout his name and watch as the car plowed into him at full speed. He heard me and looked up with the most bizarre expression. We made eye contact just before he turned to welcome the oncoming vehicle.

At impact, the car squealed to a halt. A few minutes passed before the frantic driver exited the vehicle. I knew Sang-ho was dead, and so did she.

Just as I saw the second pair of headlights speeding toward her car, I felt a heavy blow from behind. It shoved me toward the ground just like Sang-ho. I twisted and grasped blindly for the thing that had crashed into me, hoping to avoid Sang-ho's fate.

It was Mi-gyeong.

"What are you doing here?" I asked. My voice came out breathless and silent. I found I couldn't speak, yet she heard me and responded in kind.

"I don't know. I wasn't ready to leave. And I felt something was wrong."

Her body felt strange and airy, much like mine. We communicated without speaking—reading each other's thoughts, I guess, though it seemed even more elemental than that.

We both floated down toward the road, as I'd seen Sang-ho do, but I lost my grip and we drifted apart. I tried to force my way toward Mi-gyeong, but she was focused on the scene below. Even though I had seen the first car hit Sang-ho, I had no idea what was happening down there. Mi-gyeong, however, was able to tune into the minds of the people—there were three of them now—and she pieced the situation together. I caught on by listening to her thoughts.

The driver of the first car was running away from the second car. Freaked out after dragging Sang-ho along the concrete and then seeing his disfigured body, the woman ran into the field instead of getting back into her car. Mi-gyeong seemed to think the woman had seen us but that she was hiding from the occupants of the second car, which skidded to a stop just as she disappeared into the grass. Two men exited the vehicle, stalking slowly toward the woman's car and trying to make sense of the baffling scene. One of them said, "He's floating in mid-air!" I thought he was talking about me, but he was pointing at Sang-ho, who I realized was floating again because I was pulling him towards us. An appendage that looked nothing like my arm but like a thin dust spout made of shadows had stretched down to retrieve him. The other man held up a gun and boasted of the torturous things he meant to do to the woman.

Mi-gyeong tried telling the woman to run, but her shrill warning only echoed in the silence of our thoughts.

As we continued floating down toward the road, Mi-gyeong found a way to propel herself toward me. We reached out to one another, but it was unnecessary. Our thoughts drove us together, and we did not only find each other—we merged. Our bodies became one, but we didn't look human anymore. We looked like a giant black scorpion with dozens of legs, a monstrosity made from threads of the abyss we had entered. Now that Mi-gyeong was a part of me, I no longer heard or sensed her thoughts because they were indistinguishable from my own. Intense feelings of anger, resentment, revenge, and desire flooded into me like nothing I'd ever felt before. Just as

Mi-gyeong had perceived, I now fully understood what these two men meant to do to that poor woman, and it summoned such a violent need for retaliation within me—within us—that nothing could have stood in our way.

In the body of this hideous creature, Mi-gyeong and I sprouted something like fragmentary wings. We swooped down toward the man with the gun. Moving together in that immense body was like doing an elaborate dance, mentally spinning and contorting around a three-dimensional dance floor at ridiculous speeds, thrilling and terrifying at the same time. A gunshot exploded as we fell upon the man, and we felt the woman take off running from her hiding place in the grass. He continued firing, but our creature-body was not made of corporeal material. We had become the void itself, stretched beyond the limits of perception or vulnerability. The bullets passed through us, and we grabbed him, wrenching the gun-wielding limb from his body. Blood covered the road, mixing with Sang-ho's. Torturing this depraved son of Cain gave us the most satiating, rapturous sense of joy. We took his arms and legs first, keeping him alive and aware and in pain until we lopped off his head.

As the second man attempted to flee back to the car, his howls of fright filled the air. We had let go of Sang-ho's corpse, but it gaped at us with its one remaining eye as we swooped toward the second man and tore him out of the driver's seat. This man seemed less vile than the other, so he deserved a quicker death. With a long, tentacle-like arm, we swung him high overhead and brought him crashing head-first onto the road up ahead. His face shattered against the concrete, and his neck snapped with a sickening *crunch*.

Together in one body, Mi-gyeong and I laughed and cried. We thirsted for more but feared to stray too far from the blackness that still hung overhead. We were connected to it. We were a part of it. We felt we could stray if we wanted to, but then we might be irreversibly separated from our true selves. We would become this inky, blood-thirsty, god-like creature, a child of the nothingness that had drawn us in.

Mentally, we had a discussion. In a way, we both wanted to remain in that form. The sensation of power, confidence, and possibilities at our fingertips was an elixir like nothing we could imagine finding in our daily lives. But we knew it was unnatural, and that frightened us.

Disturbing though it was, the sight of the dead bodies almost convinced us to abandon everything we knew and remain like that. Sang-ho's crushed skull, the gunman's dismembered torso, the third man's broken neck—looking upon them felt like being sexually aroused, or being a drug addict itching for the fix in his pocket. It became a compulsion neither of us could ignore.

I felt Mi-gyeong leaning into it, and I started to follow. We began to pull away from the void, emerging into a new life, a new purpose, bound together and immensely powerful. We could go anywhere and do anything, consuming anyone who crossed our path. The woman from the first car was still nearby; we could sense her. There were a few others as well, and more coming. However, just before we broke away in pursuit of the woman, I got a better look at her car.

The Maryland license plate caught my attention because I was born and raised outside Baltimore. As I paused to look closer, I felt Mi-gyeong trying to pull me away, but I drew us nearer to the car. Though the night was pitch dark and our blackness leaked into it, both cars were still running, their headlights shining and interior lights glowing. The car was an older model, early 2000s maybe, and it seemed familiar in an uncomfortable way, like when you can't remember something important because a part of you wants to forget. The number on the license plate seemed familiar, too, but most license plates are like that. Then, I realized it was a 2005 Ford Taurus.

Silver. I had been inside that car. Gone on road trips in that car. Received my first backseat blowjob in that car.

It belonged to Maggie Garrick.

Before I came to Korea, Maggie and I had been together for about five years. As with so many relationships, we had great times together, but the thrill wore thin and we moved on. Somehow, my wife had gotten it into her head that I still had feelings for Maggie. That was what we'd been fighting about the past several weeks. That was why I'd been sleeping on the sofa. That was why she'd gone out of the blue to visit her aunt in Jeonju and, unfortunately, discovered her aunt's gored body, driving the wedge even deeper between us.

Realizing all these things at once, I suddenly forgot about the three dead bodies and the addictive pull to sniff out more. My mind—and therefore Mi-gyeong's mind—was overcome with thoughts of the Han River, Yeouido, my wife and our ongoing argument, my job, our apartment, and the Seogang Bridge. I got flashes of Mi-gyeong's life, too. Her friends, an abusive family, college entrance preparations, and her thwarted attempt on her own life. Against Mi-gyeong's wild struggle to stay, these combined thoughts convinced me to retreat back into the void.

I woke up on the sofa, naked, drenched, and shivering. While I gazed around in bafflement, I heard the bedroom door open. My wife came into the living room. Her eyes went wide when she saw me. Instead of asking if I was okay, she scoffed and said, "You asshole. Drunk and thinking about your ex again?"

I just stared at her, shaking my head idiotically. "No... No..."

After drying myself off, I threw on some clothes and laid down. My clothes from the previous day lay in a sopping pile on the bathroom floor. It felt like I hadn't slept more than a few minutes. I tried to calm my mind, but everything I'd seen was still clear in my memory, refusing to fade away like dreams usually do. Ten minutes later, I gave up. I hopped off the sofa and ran to the window. I had to see it. I felt I would never be able to rest if I didn't see it at that moment.

A clear and beautiful day greeted me. The buildings of Yeouido stood tall across the river, reflecting the morning sunlight. Chuckling to myself, I shouted to my wife, "It's okay! It's still there!"

"What?" she said, annoyed.

"Yeouido is still there!"

I made coffee and sat down, relieved and never more pleased at the sight of those buildings. As I drank my coffee, I remembered all the shocking things I'd seen, heard, and felt during the night. The suffocating blackness had been a hundred times more dense than the black hole in my coffee mug. Recalling the country road and Maggie's car and the three mutilated bodies, an unsettling restlessness began to creep back. Why did it all feel so real?

By the time I finished my coffee, I knew that seeing Yeouido from afar would not be enough to ease my mind. Same as the night before, I desperately needed to see it up close.

Outside, the weather was pleasantly warm. Hardly a cloud in the brilliant autumn sky. Gwanak Mountain stood in sharp clarity behind the Yeouido skyline. I followed the same route as always, down one street, up another, and through the tunnel underpass. People were walking, jogging, and cruising past on bicycles. A young couple sat on one of the benches with their elderly grandparents.

Off to my left, the lush greenery of Bam Island rose out of the river while the water of the Han looked clearer than usual. Satisfied, I turned to head home so I could take care of a few things before work.

Before I reached the tunnel entrance, I noticed a crowd gathered along the riverside railing. They were looking out into the river or across it, once again reminding me of things I would rather have forgotten. With the briefest hesitation, I walked along the bike path to join them.

Several police boats had gathered near the western edge of Bam Island. On the muddy shoreline lay a body. The boats got as close as they could, but several police officers had to get out and wade onto the silt.

From behind me came a chaotic burst of yelling and shouting. A family raced up the bike lane. The adult children tried to hold back their mother, who broke away toward the crowd. She pushed through the people to reach the railing, determined to climb over it into the swashing water below. Her children, a man and a woman, caught up and pulled her back down. She fell to her knees and wailed,

"Sang-ho-ya! Sang-ho! Sang-ho...Sang-ho-ya..."

I stared at her in disbelief. My legs felt weak as I flushed with terror. When I looked back out to the river, the cops were lifting the lifeless body into a boat. They were too far away to see clearly, but I knew—it was a man in a cheap suit and white shirt, his face crushed on one side. I just knew it.

I took several deep breaths, trying to calm myself. I kept telling myself how ludicrous it sounded and that it could not be possible. There must be hundreds of men named Sang-ho. It's not an uncommon name...

Near the edge of the group, I heard a choked gasp. Peering through the tightly packed faces, I saw another impossibility standing not three meters away. She kept looking in shock from the old woman bawling by the railing to the corpse being maneuvered into the boat. Then she saw me.

Mi-gyeong.

As her eyes locked with mine, both of our jaws dropped. Just like me, she ceased noticing anything else. It felt like we were back in the darkness, merged together as one, experiencing life and death and pleasure and torture, as one.

The old woman shrieked and hollered as her family tried to

drag her away. Both Mi-gyeong and I turned to watch. The police had finally managed to get the body into the boat. All the boats sped away toward the southern bank. The crowd began to disperse. Mi-gyeong and I resumed staring at one another. The creeping fear I'd been trying to stave off clamped tightly around my throat. I felt strangled with fright. I needed to look across the river to see Yeouido again, but I was afraid it wouldn't be there. Or if it was, then I'd turn back and Mi-gyeong would be gone.

I took a step forward. She looked away, not toward the receding boats or Yeouido, but toward the Seogang Bridge. Shaking her head, she went pale and tried to step back but tripped over a woman's foot. She caught herself, apologizing to the woman without ever taking her eyes off me. I held my hands up, a gentle but imperative greeting. She shook her head again, just a subtle wiggle. Even though she never moved her lips, I could have sworn I heard her voice.

No, please don't...

She turned and fled, pushing through the people who had yet to move on from the river's edge.

I chased after her, but she was too quick. She kept turning back, and seeing me seemed to give her fresh bursts of energy. I was already falling behind when she approached the walkway leading away from the river and up to a small park. As I crossed the path, a middle-aged man on a bicycle sped by and clipped my shin. It knocked me to the ground. The man managed to keep his balance, but he slammed on his brakes and threw down his bike in a rage, storming over to me and drawing a crowd as he screamed vulgar names. But I barely heard him. I rubbed my leg where his tire had struck and looked around for Mi-gyeong. Eventually, a few other bikers pulled the man away before he started throwing punches, not to protect me but only to berate him for dropping his bike in the bike lane.

I got away and limped up the walkway. The park was full of

couples and families, but I saw no sign of Mi-gyeong. She was gone.

My leg is still in a lot of pain. I think my ankle might be sprained. When I got home, my wife had already left for work. It wasn't long before my boss started calling. I ignored her calls and messages.

It's evening now. I haven't been able to budge from the window all day. Every now and then, I feel a rush of dizzying terror when I see something that might be fog or mist cut across the river. I wish I knew of some way to find Mi-gyeong. I scoured social media but came up with nothing. I thought about calling the police to ask about Sang-ho, but what would I say when they started asking questions? I'm still contemplating whether I should try to get ahold of Maggie Garrick, but if my wife finds out, she'll kill me.

Speaking of my wife—she should be home by now, but she's not.

My place in the world feels fractured and incomplete. I feel like I don't belong here. Like I don't belong anywhere except the generous, suffocating embrace of that tantalizing darkness.

LEATHERMAN

Stephen sat cross-legged on a flattened cardboard box. He'd found it out front of a house on 98th Street. It had been stuffed with tissue paper, and someone had written *Kittens, Free* in black magic marker. Either passersby had taken all the kittens, or they'd climbed out to chance a life on the streets. The tissue paper had been soiled with cat piss, so he got rid of it. A trace scent remained on the cardboard, but it was still a nicer box than the one he'd been using for a bed.

After carrying the box back to where he'd been staying on 81st, he flattened it out. Instead of replacing his filthy, soiled bed in the stairwell right away, he laid the new cardboard right in the center of the alley. At this time of the evening, the sun would be coming down. For about ten minutes, it would shine in the gap between the two buildings opposite, filling his alley with intense warmth and light—the best part of Stephen's day.

So, he sat like a monk, emptying his mind of everything except the life-giving, life-affirming sunlight. He forgot about all the terrible things he'd seen, all the screams, and that final harrowing act that had driven him away from home for good.

He did not want to remember how he ended up on 81st Street in Brooklyn or all the immoral things he had to do to survive. All he wanted was to remain here. The sunken basement entryway he holed up in felt safe. The red brick building across the alley had become as familiar as a bedroom wall. Even the odor from the dumpsters had grown on him. He had gathered an admirable collection of necessities—a stained but plush pillow, several tattered quilts, a collection of dented canned goods, and a rusty Leatherman multi-tool to open them with. He even had a stuffed animal that looked like Peppercorn, his family's aged Border Collie—Peppy, as they usually called her.

And he had moments like this—cloudless days when the sun filled his alley like a gift from God. It was a blessing, however temporary, reminding him that poverty was a small price to pay for what he had done.

Grateful for what he had, Stephen shut his eyes, soaking in the rays and murmuring a prayer he said every day at this time.

"Please, God, please. I accept any punishment you choose to inflict...but I still hear their screams. Please, I beg you, please make them stop. Please..."

When he opened his eyes, a dark figure stood silhouetted at the head of the alleyway. The sun blasted the figure from behind. For a brief moment, Stephen thought God had come to answer his prayer. Although, the Reaper seemed more likely— just aching to end Stephen's miserable existence when he had finally found a place that felt like home. Or it could be the police again, finally coming to haul him away. They never offered help or advice, never told the homeless where it was okay to stay, only that they could not stay where they wanted.

Instead of continuing along the sidewalk, the figure stood peering between the buildings. Stephen realized the person was looking right at him, but all Stephen could see was a dark outline.

When the figure started to walk into the alley, Stephen

grew tense. He glanced around in search of something to defend himself with. A trash can lid, a brick, or an old bottle would be his most immediately available weapons. His Leatherman was hidden in a crack on the landing.

He could get up and run or remain seated where he was, meditating over the setting sun and grateful for whatever crumbs life might toss his way, even if that meant punishment.

"Hey-yo! Steve-o the Schizo! How you doin', my man?"

Steve-o the Schizo...

Stephen had heard that name before. At first, he was flattered. It meant he'd lived between these two buildings long enough to have earned a nickname from the neighbors. But when he thought about what the name actually meant, it didn't sit so well anymore.

The figure came closer, still keeping a good ten feet of space between them but close enough that Stephen should have been able to see his face. Still, all he saw were the brilliant rays of the sun illuminating the man from behind.

"Are you real?" asked Stephen.

"Whadd'you mean?" the figure laughed. "I'd better be real. If I ain't real, my *um-ma* is gonna be fuckin' pissed."

"Um...ma?"

"It means Mom, Steve-o."

"That's not real..."

That laugh again, high-pitched and excitable. "It is! It's what we call our mothers where I come from!"

"Where?"

"I'm from a city called Jeonju, in—"

"No...that's not real. You're not real."

"Steve-o, come on, man. Don't do me like that. I am real, and I'm for real. Look, we've met before. Right out here in this alley. Don't you remember me?"

"Travis?"

"Naw, man. I'm Kevin. Kevin Park. I live in this building right here. Apartment 401."

Raising his hand to shield his eyes, Stephen said, "I can't see you. You're like a...like a shadow."

The figure turned toward the sunlight and shielded his eyes, too. He stepped to the side nearest his building without getting much closer to Stephen. Looking down, he saw he'd put his foot in a pile of something that looked like vomit.

"Shit..." groaned the figure. "Gross..."

"Who? Me?"

"Not you, this shit on the..." He pointed down as he hopped back, wiping his shoe on the concrete. "You sat down right next to that. Didn't you even see it? Can't you smell it? Oh my God, there's blood in it..."

"What?"

"Look... Wait, did you...? Hey, Steve-o, you alright?"

"Are you the one who left me the bottle of medicine?"

"Medicine? Nah, that wasn't me."

"I drank it all," Stephen said wistfully. "It made me feel... funny. Like floating and sleeping at the same time. Dreaming. Do you have any more?"

Now that the figure had moved to the side, Stephen tried to see his face again. Even with the sunlight directly illuminating him, his features appeared fuzzy and indistinct.

"I told you, I didn't give it to you. I don't even know what you're talking about."

"It didn't taste very good. But sometimes, the best-tasting things are bad for us. My mom used to say that—"

"Your *um-ma.*"

Startled by the interruption, Stephen stared at the blurry-faced figure with an unsettling, squint-eyed stare.

"Hey, Steve-o, come on, man. Don't make fun like that."

"You're not even real. My mom used to say the best things

are bad for us, so I'm not supposed to have more medicine. But do you know what my dad said?"

"What'd your dad say?"

"He said, '*Shut your fuckin' mouth, bitch!*' And he said it every day. Then, one day, he said, '*You goddamn nosy slut, you just couldn't mind your business. Now I've got to shut you up for good!*' After that, Mom left and didn't come home anymore. It was just me and Dad...and the ones he brought to the basement."

"That sounds, uh...creepy as fuck."

"Dad said they were his friends."

"Where's your dad now?"

"He's... He's not here."

"I know that. But do you know where he is?"

"I left and didn't come home anymore, just like my mom. Now, this is my home. I like it here."

"But don't you want a real place to live? What happens when winter comes, man? You'll freeze to death out here. There are places you can go." The figure squatted down, but when he got a whiff of the sludgy, gooey puddle, he shot back up in a hurry. "I mean, shelters for people like...people with no place to live. You can sleep with a roof over your head and a hot meal. There're people to help you, too."

"I have a roof," Stephen sounded offended. He pointed at the sunken landing where he slept. Then, indicating the sheet of cardboard beneath him, he added proudly, "And a new bed."

"That is not a home, Steve-o. If it storms some night, you'll drown down there, and this bed of yours is gonna disintegrate."

"Are you...kicking me out?"

"Nah, of course not, my man. You can stay here as long as you want for all I care." The man glanced around nervously and lowered his voice. "It's the super you need to be worried about. Mr Lorenzo doesn't like, uh...stragglers hanging around out front of the building."

Stephen stared at him with an idiotic expression and glanced up at the buildings on either side of them.

"Or in the alley," added the man. "I think he's already called the cops about you."

"I saw the police."

"I know. They came here, didn't they? That's what I said. And it was Lorenzo who called them. What'd they say to you?"

"I saw them. On the TV."

"That's not what I—"

"They said my dad was dead and that I killed him with garden shears. But they were wrong, I—"

"What?" screeched the man. His features were becoming more defined. He looked shocked or frightened or sick, and a bit jittery, like he didn't want to be there anymore.

"It wasn't garden shears. And then I used his tools. The tools he used to make those people in the basement scream. And my mom."

"What the fuck...? Steve-o, are you serious? Did that really happen?"

"The policemen? Well, I don't know if that was real. It was on TV."

"You don't have a TV, man."

"I know," Stephen stated simply, staring at the figure. "I saw it at Huntsman's. Sometimes, the man lets me inside after hours. He gives me bagels and juice, and we watch TV together. I don't drink the coffee..."

The man let out a deep breath and smiled, nodding in understanding. Obscured by his dark, shaggy hair, his eyes appeared rather shifty. His skin was smooth and sallow.

"But the policemen who came here," Stephen continued abruptly, "they told me I can stay as long as I keep my stuff over there." He pointed at the sunken landing again. "They were real. But you're not."

The man started pacing and laughing in that same whiny, high-pitched laugh. "Shit. Steve-o, man, you really had me freaked for a second. I thought you really… No, never mind. Look, I better—"

"Hey." Stephen still hadn't moved from his cross-legged position. "Can you get me more?"

"More what?"

"Medicine."

"I told you, I didn't—" The man glanced down the alley toward the street and heaved a bothered sigh. "Yeah, I can get you more. Do you know what it was? Still have the bottle?"

Without a word, Stephen stood up and crept toward his landing. He ducked into it, stooping to rummage through his things. Amazingly, he did it all without making a sound. He always tried to be as silent as possible because loud noises frightened him. Not all loud noises. Some, like traffic, were comforting. The sounds of engines, horns, squeaking belts, and blaring radios reminded him of the cars that had taken him away from home, away from his dad, away from what he'd done. Kind strangers and their cars brought him here to New York City.

He grabbed two items from among his limited array of possessions. One, he shoved into the kangaroo pocket of his stained pullover sweatshirt. With the other item in both hands, he returned and retook his place on the cardboard. He held out the empty bottle of NyQuil but then abruptly pulled it back.

"But I can't give it to you."

"Why not?"

"Because you're not real."

"I'm real, Steve-o. I swear. Look, I'll prove it, alright? Give me the bottle. If it falls to the ground, then I must not be real.

But if it doesn't, well, then I have to be a living person, right?"

Stephen gazed at him skeptically. After considering this for a minute, he held out the bottle again. The figure took it. Stephen waited, staring at the man's feet and tilting his ear toward the ground. Suddenly, he looked up, shielding his eyes.

"I know you," he said.

"That's what I've been trying to tell you! Do you remember my name? I just told you. Come on, think..."

"Where were you?"

"I was at work all day. Just on my way home—"

"No, not today..." Stephen shoved his hands into the kangaroo pocket. He seemed anxious as he fiddled with something. "Two days ago. And yesterday. You weren't here."

"How the hell do you know that?" the man asked with a strained laugh. He gazed down at the NyQuil bottle, only peering at Stephen from the corner of his eye.

"I watch," Stephen said cryptically. "I see you people come and go. I watch, and I listen. People always come home. Someone scares me in the night, every night. I don't think I can take it anymore. I don't want to leave, but...but the sounds frighten me. Like you. You didn't come home two nights ago, and you looked guilty when you arrived late last night. I saw you come home, and I was afraid. Because you've done something bad..." He paused, raised his eyes, and stared directly at the man as he hissed, "...*Kevin Park.*"

Kevin's laughter choked off at once. He glanced up quickly to see Stephen's eyes locked unblinkingly on him. Shuddering, Kevin looked away again.

"Where were you, Kevin?" Suddenly, Stephen's voice sounded friendly again, almost passively curious, like banter from a co-worker or a bartender.

"I had to go to Maryland."

"To do something bad. I can...smell it."

"How can you smell anything when you stink like a dumpster?" scoffed Kevin.

"Must have been really bad... Should I tell the police when they come back?"

"No! No, it was nothing..." Kevin tried to laugh it off, but he sounded like a sick donkey, or maybe a goat. "I just...my cousin asked me to do her a favor, and she... Wait, what do you mean the cops are coming back? Were they looking for me?"

A smile slid across Stephen's lips like a nightcrawler. It stretched wide, his mouth opening to show brown, plaque-covered teeth, and he started to titter. A ticklish, evasive laughter. "I know you. I know you. I know what you've done."

"Get outta here..." Kevin said, rubbing the back of his head and averting his eyes toward the street.

"I do. You hurt her, didn't you? You hurt her because... because you wanted to stick your little pecker into her! Didn't you? Didn't you, Kevin Park?"

"Shut up!" Kevin shouted, his eyes flashing and fists clenched as he stepped toward Stephen. "I didn't do anything like that! I swear!"

Above them, a window screeched open, then another. Kevin looked up and saw two people peering into the alley, one from each building. The person from his building was Mrs Cazares in 303. When Kevin waved at her, Stephen suddenly looked up and waved, too. Even after she pulled her head back inside, Stephen continued glaring up at the window.

"Look, Steve-o, I don't—"

"It's Stephen, actually. Stephen Tinkerman."

"Sorry, Stephen... I don't know what you're talking about. I never took advantage of a woman in my—"

"You're lying. I can smell it, just like I could smell it on Daddy." All this time, Stephen had been fidgeting with the object in his kangaroo pocket. Now, it became more pronounced. It almost looked like he was masturbating, but Kevin could see his hands were in the pocket, not in his pants.

"How do you... Alright! Okay! One time. It only happened once, but that was a long time ago. In college! She was drunk, and so was I! It could happen to anybody! I felt like shit about it the next day, okay? I still feel like shit about it! But that's not what happened in Maryland! Nothing like that! I swear!"

"Something worse."

"Jesus, man," Kevin started backing away. "You really are some kinda freak schizo..." He turned away, stumbling as he tried to avoid the patch of vomit, and hurried out of the alley.

"Hey, Kevin Park," Stephen called after him.

When Kevin glanced back, he saw Stephen pulling something from his sweatshirt pocket. At first, he couldn't tell what it was. But when Stephen unfolded it, the last rays of sunlight from between the buildings glinted off the blade.

"Kevin Park from 401." Stephen waved the Leatherman blade enticingly. Then, with a series of curious slicing motions, he slowly raised his arm, pointing the blade at the fourth floor of Kevin's building.

Frozen stiff in the middle of the alley, Kevin repeatedly looked from Stephen to 81st Street, unable to decide what to do. No one was out on the street. No one passing by. No heads hung from the windows above to watch this little drama unfold. No witnesses.

"What do you want?" Kevin asked in a hoarse voice. His legs felt so weak that he didn't think he could climb the four flights to his apartment.

"Tell me what you did."

"Then you'll leave me alone?"

Instead of answering, Stephen laid the open Leatherman on his cardboard mat.

After another glance back at the street, Kevin took a few tentative steps closer. He didn't come nearly as close as before.

"Promise?" said Kevin.

"I just want the screams to stop."

"What?"

"Bad people like you make people scream." Stephen's face wrenched into an awful wincing grimace. He covered his ears, and his lips separated in a silent, pained bellow.

Shaking his head, Kevin took a few steps closer. He squatted down at the foot of the cardboard. "I'm not bad, Steve-o...Stephen. Honest. I just..."

"What did you do?"

"I told you. My cousin asked me for a favor. Right? She has some sort of grudge or something against this chick she's never even met. She offered me money, okay? And I need it. Like, I need it really badly, or I'm going to be evicted. I'll be living in the alley with you."

"It's not so bad," mumbled Stephen. "Except for the screams."

"So my cousin wanted me to go to this town called Mount Airy in Maryland and find this girl—"

Stephen abruptly grabbed the Leatherman. Kevin's hands flew up like a cop had just drawn his gun.

"No, no, no! It wasn't like that! All she wanted me to do was find the girl and show her."

"Show her?"

Kevin pulled his phone out of his pocket. "You know, video call? FaceTime? Just turn on the camera and get her in the shot. I didn't even have to be close to the woman. Never came within five meters."

"Why?"

"It doesn't matter. I didn't hurt her. All I did was FaceTime with my cousin and *um-ma*."

"Your mom?"

"Yeah! See, you got it!"

"I meant, why? Why your mom?"

"I don't know. I never even asked, okay? I just needed the money. My cousin doesn't like the girl, probably for some stupid reason, and my mom is a shaman, so, you know..."

"No." Stephen shrugged. "That's not real."

"Yeah, I'm with you on that. People like that, they're crazy, and my mom especially. I never believed in all that hoodoo shit she does. How do you think I felt as a kid, huh? With her doing animal sacrifices and shit all the time. The screams of innocent animals. The blood. People moaning and howling and acting like possessed maniacs. Right out back of our house! That's why I left that fuckin' shithole, Steve-o. Sorry, Stephen."

Finally, Stephen folded the Leatherman shut, the blade disappeared, and he put the tool back in his kangaroo pocket. He didn't say anything but just stared at the cardboard. After a while, his neck cranked back so he could stare up at Kevin's building with wide, bloodshot eyes.

"Me, too," muttered Stephen, nodding repeatedly as though someone was speaking to him.

Kevin stared in dumb, shocked silence.

"When I was a child," Stephen went on absently, "and a teenager, and a grown-up, I heard their screams. Always there. The hysterical shrieks of the innocent. The ghostly wails of the dead. His *friends*. I saw the blood, too. I smelled it. I smelled them. Downstairs. The basement. Just like I smelled his lies. I made them stop—the lies and the smell. But I made more blood. And the screams. I couldn't stop them. I still hear the screams. Every night. I hear them. I'm haunted. I'm cursed. You did that, Kevin. You made that woman scream!"

Stephen pointed up at the window that had opened a little while earlier. He stretched as far as he could without standing up, pointing so hard that his hand and arm began to tremble. His jaw was clenched, veins on his neck popped out, and his face turned scarlet.

"No, Stephen. I know that scream you hear. That's not in your head. It's real. Everyone hears it."

"I know..."

"But it's okay. She's just dreaming. No one hurt her, alright? I promise. I talked to her myself. She's been having bad dreams, that's all. Nothing to worry about."

Shaking his head in defiance, Stephen dropped his arm and pointed at Kevin just as intently. His other hand slipped into the kangaroo pocket again to fidget with the Leatherman.

"It's you," Stephen barked, shaking his head. "She screams because of people like you and Daddy. Everyone calls me Steve-o the Schizo, but I don't hear voices. Only screams. I just want the screams to stop. They follow me. They scare me. They become me. I made them stop once. Do you know how?"

Kevin stood up and backed away, muttering incoherently. "No...I...no..."

"I sliced my murdering Daddy's neck with his own tools. It wasn't the garden shears like they said. It was his leather shears. Sliced his neck, gouged out his eyes, and cut his hands off. You know what I did then? I got the pistol from the night-stand in his bedroom and put five bullets in his chest, one in his brain. Then I let him go. Do you understand now? Do you understand what needs to be done?"

With his mouth hanging open in idiotic fear, Kevin shook his head. All he understood was that the bum living in their alley was fucking nuts.

"That's why I love my Leatherman," Stephen explained, taking the tool out of his pocket again. He opened the blade and smiled as he held it up. "Because I used his leather shears."

"Who...who...who did you let go?"

"The one Daddy was about to kill. Travis. We ran away together. But do you know what?"

"What?"

"The screams came back. They turned Travis into a bad

guy, just like Daddy. And like you. It's alright," Stephen shrugged. "My Leatherman knows what to do."

As Kevin left the alley, he shivered at the sound of Stephen weeping and muttering about the screams. When he reached the street, he realized he was still holding onto the NyQuil bottle, crushed out of shape by his tense grip. Kevin was so disturbed by the encounter with Stephen that he had forgotten why he had it. He dropped the bottle in the trash bin out front of his building and went inside.

HEIGH HO, GOTTA GO

Aside from the cockroaches in the second stall, the women's restroom was empty when Irene Marquardt came in. Two of the three overhead fluorescent bulbs were burnt out. By the looks of it, the floor hadn't been scrubbed in ten years. The trash can was overflowing, both sinks had rust stains, there was a used hypodermic needle in the corner, and the mirror above the sink on the right had been shattered.

The hole in the door of the second stall, where the lock should have been, was a sign to use the first stall. Too flustered to register this detail, Irene almost missed it. Had her subconscious overlooked this hole, she would have gone for the second stall and been greeted by the cockroaches—then her visit to this restroom might have ended a whole lot differently.

Inside the first stall, Irene engaged the lock. The satisfying metallic clink drew from her a deep exhalation as she sank onto the toilet lid. She buried her face in her hands, forcing a scream back down her throat. After a minute or so, she opened her eyes and saw a single cockroach wander beneath the divider. She swiped at it with her sneaker, spooking it back into the second stall. Though she would have preferred to hunker down in the stall for a while and try to get a grip on herself, the insect creeped her out just enough to hurry her along.

She had not come into the restroom to use the toilet. She'd used one an hour ago when she stopped for a bite to eat outside Lexington. The Wendy's facilities had been much nicer but still a far cry from home. The farther she got, the less likely it seemed she would ever enjoy the comforts of her own bathroom again, and the more it hurt. She thought she had to be into Ohio by now, but she hadn't paid much attention to road signs since before she entered Kentucky. Fortunately, she had paused at that T-junction to contemplate her choices and glanced down at the dashboard, noticing the empty fuel indicator. Her groan of frustration was placated when she looked up and saw the sign dead ahead—*ExxonMobil, 2 miles*—directing her to head west.

Since she had no intention of stopping again before Cleveland, it was better to ensure her bladder was empty. After double-checking that the lock was secure, she lifted the toilet lid and pulled down her acid-wash jeans. It wasn't urgent, but she had taken a coffee-to-go from Wendy's, so she would have had to stop sooner or later.

Tears welled up in her eyes while she waited. Before she left that afternoon, Ted had all but told her not to come home. Caleb and Liz were right there in the living room, gape-mouthed by the uncommon sight of their father shouting, their mother crying. Seething, Ted had given her the ultimatum with a serrated edge to his voice that Irene had never heard before, although she'd actually laid the foundations the year before.

Seriously, what were the chances? That Ted's brother's new wife had been promoted to regional manager for the New England states just weeks before the yearly conference? Irene knew there was a new manager. The previous manager, Hank Tinkerman, had died suddenly, apparently murdered by his own adult son, who had then disappeared. She heard that there were other extenuating circumstances, but she'd never looked into it. The whole thing had been too disturbing, and she didn't want to think about it in connection with her work. However, if she had only bothered to get to know Allen's new wife, she might have learned that Claire had been managing the Rochester branch for five years and that she'd kept her maiden name after the marriage. Then, after they sent her to Boston to take over Tinkerman's job, Irene would have expected to run into her at company-wide events.

So, that was why Allen and Claire moved to Massachusetts. At last year's conference in St Louis, the bitch, Claire La Palma, had seen Irene with Oren Wilder, the regional manager for the Midwest. Irene and Oren had come into the conference hall already drunk and hanging all over each other. Claire must have seen them leave together on their way up to Irene's room. Instead of speaking discreetly with Irene about the indiscretion, Claire called her husband, who naturally called to inform big brother Ted.

Finally, Irene got the waterworks flowing. There wasn't much, but it was better to get it out of the way now than to stop at another rundown gas station in the middle of nowhere.

"Shit."

No toilet paper. Irene felt the scream rising in her throat like churning nausea. She choked it back down. In a sudden hurry to get out of there, she yanked her pants up, slammed down the toilet seat, and flushed. When she tried to unlatch the rusted lock, it wouldn't budge. The scream started rising faster. Squeezing her eyes shut, she slammed her fist into the door.

Click.

The lock unlatched itself. Irene took a deep breath and stepped out.

Two sinks—one with no mirror and one with no faucet. She stepped up to the mirrorless sink on the right, expecting no running water. Surprisingly, the water flow was just fine. Cranking the hot handle even lent the biting cold water a bit of warmth. She let it run over her hands while she stared at the broken mirror. Half the glass was lying in the sink, and the other half remained on the wall, segregated by a chaotic web of lines. Her reflection shone back at her, distorted and disfigured, a monstrous version of herself. She realized it was a pretty accurate representation of how she had been feeling since the showdown with Ted a few hours earlier.

When she returned home from last year's conference, Ted told her he knew everything and threatened to leave her. Not wanting to wake the kids, he hadn't screamed that time. He hadn't even seemed all that angry, just disappointed. Heartbroken. Irene knew she fucked up. She didn't even know why she did it, but she did do it, and she couldn't talk her way out of it. Somehow, she convinced Ted to give her another chance. She spent the whole year doing everything in her power to repair the marriage and regain his trust.

And she thought she had. When this year's conference came around, she assumed they'd healed. She never even considered not going to the conference. How could she? She was well on her way to making vice president. She hadn't even thought about—

No. That wasn't true. She had been thinking about Oren Wilder. Two weeks before the conference, she had a series of dreams. Fucking Oren. Sucking Oren. Dirty, drunken sex, just like the year before. She didn't want to cheat on Ted again, but she had been thinking about it. Thinking about it in a way that seemed—as much as she hated to admit it—almost inevitable. Then, the Monday before the conference, she received two emails, a company-wide one announcing the retirement of

Betty Flagstaff and another private one informing her of her impending promotion to VP.

For the rest of that week, she'd been riding high, in the best mood since last year's blowup with Ted. Mostly, it was because of the promotion. She'd been working toward this for seventeen years. However, there was a shadow in the back of her mind, looking forward to and even planning a low-key but raunchy celebration with Oren Wilder.

The bar of soap was crusty. There appeared to be several pubic hairs embedded in it. Irene made a throaty gurgle of disgust as she let the water rinse them off before soaping her hands. As she did, she gazed at the glass shards in the sink. On top, a large, jagged piece was flipped over so the reflective surface was face down. The coated back blended in with the filthy porcelain. The shard was long, maybe eight inches, razor-sharp, and pointed like a hunting knife.

Irene scrubbed her hands more fiercely than necessary. She rinsed them off and then, with the water still running, flipped over the shard.

Why hadn't she mentioned the conference to Ted? Was she intentionally trying to hide it from him? Had she been trying to avoid the inevitable recurrence of last year's fight? Was she trying to shield him or herself? Or the kids? It came up in conversation at least once, but maybe she hadn't been clear about her intention—her obligation—to attend. She had told him about the promotion, of course, and tried to ignore the fact that he didn't seem all too thrilled. Unless they were in one of their couple's therapy sessions with Dr Denise Zimmer, he tended to become reticent whenever the topic of her job came up. Met with Ted's less-than-enthusiastic reaction, she stopped herself from saying any more on the subject, such as, *They're going to make it official at the conference this Friday.*

Had she left that out on purpose? Was her mind intentionally dodging a minefield?

Her reflection in the shard looked hollow and defeated. Her mascara had run. Her eyes were wrenched open like she'd seen a ghost. The water pouring out of the faucet distorted her face, making her features bent and grotesque, a changeling. She wrapped her fingers around it and picked it up.

The notion of continuing the rest of the way to Cleveland drew a knot in her stomach. The scream had left her throat and found its way up into her brain. She heard it, bellowing curses and hate at the reflection in the broken glass.

Ted hadn't said much to her for two days before she left. She didn't realize what was wrong until her bag was packed and she found him waiting in the living room. Caleb and Liz were watching an old Disney animation. Ted was just standing beside the sofa with his arms crossed, staring right at her as she came down the hall with her duffel bag.

Somehow, he knew.

All he said was, "Is he going to be there?"

"Ted, I have t—"

Heigh Ho, Heigh Ho...

The kids were following their dad's lead—staring at Irene and waiting for an explanation. When the seven dwarfs suddenly broke into their obnoxious song, Irene, Ted, and the kids all turned sharply toward the television.

Then, the shouting began.

Four more hours on the road felt like a stretch in solitary confinement. She couldn't go home, and she couldn't deal with the silence of a hotel room. She didn't want anything to do with Oren Wilder, not anymore. What good was a promotion to vice president if her family left her?

When Irene lifted the shard above the faucet, the water slid off it. A few drops remained. They looked like tears on her cheeks. She moaned and looked up, where she was met with the crooked-faced thing in the mirror. She had five black-hole eyes and a monstrously oversized forehead. Her teeth were cracked. A psychotic grin tilted jaggedly across her face. No nose.

Was this the monster responsible for destroying her family?

Irene wrapped her hand around the thicker end of the shard. She raised the pointed end to her neck, touching it there with just enough pressure to raise a globule of blood.

Ted had screamed for ten minutes straight. Irene couldn't get a word in. Even if he had left a space for her, she was too shocked by his tirade to respond. Not because he was berating her with such vicious language in front of the kids, but because everything he said was true. It was like he'd been reading her mind for two weeks. Like he'd seen into her dreams—fucking, sucking. He didn't give a shit about her promotion or her career or her goddamn reputation. He needed her word. He needed to trust her. Caleb started to weep. Liz buried her head under her Snow White blanket. Ted kept right on going, breaking down with sickening logic and frightening accuracy how the past year had been a sham. Everything Irene had said and done had been leading up to that precise confrontation, and she blew it. All their progress was worth nothing more than a fifty-cent apology card reading *Sorry, not sorry.*

She had already made her choice. Ted knew that, but he was willing to offer her one last chance because, other than packing her bag, she hadn't acted on it yet.

If she walked out the door and went to the conference, Ted would be in California with the kids by the time she returned. Plenty of room at his folks' place and plenty of job opportunities in his line of work. Divorce and custody papers would be in her hands by the end of the week. She would never see Caleb and Liz again.

Or, she could set down her bag, double down on her shallow promises of the previous year, and spend the weekend with him and the kids.

Irene pressed a little harder, grunting at the pain. Her hand started to shake. The tiny poke became an incision. Blood dribbled down the reflective surface and collected in the creases of her fingers.

"The promotion, Ted. I have to—"

"That's not what this is about! Stop bullshitting us!"

Liz started wailing beneath her blanket. Caleb, only six years old, stared at his mom with something like resentment, as though the situation unfolding in the living room was just a part of the movie, and his mom was the wicked queen.

Mirror, mirror on the wall...

Irene couldn't remember what she said after that, or if she said anything at all. She had no recollection of making a conscious decision, nor did she recall saying goodbye to her children. Next thing she knew, she was speeding out of Nashville on her way to Cleveland.

Now, several foggy hours later, she was in the restroom of an Exxon somewhere in southern Ohio with a shard of glass jabbed into her throat, no more than an inch from her carotid artery.

Mirror, Mirror in my neck...

Pain crept along her flesh like an anesthetic. Numbing fear plunged through her. She couldn't even face herself, so how would she ever face the life she'd left in ruins? She couldn't answer for her mistakes or her uncontrolled desires, but neither could she face the shame of bleeding out on the floor of this moldy, foul-smelling restroom.

What she wanted was to combust. Her husband had pumped her full of fuel, and now she wanted to burn it off. The shard—it didn't belong in her neck. It should be piercing Claire La Palma's eyes, protruding from her brother-in-law's windpipe, slicing Oren Wilder's scrotum off, stabbing into Ted's beating heart. She wanted to paint the walls of this backwoods filling station restroom red, but not with her own blood.

Mirror, Mirror in my hand...

A faint but shrill note of music distracted Irene. It seemed to be getting closer. And it sounded painfully familiar.

The door burst open. Irene glanced up into the cracked mirror to see a woman enter absentmindedly. She had dark hair and looked to be around thirty. Even though the look in her eyes was dejected, her expression seemed placid and at peace as she came in whistling a joyous, optimistic tune. It was a melody Irene soon recognized and the last thing she wanted to hear.

Heigh Ho, Heigh Ho...

The seven dwarfs singing about coming home from fucking work.

Irene watched through the webbed mirror until the door shut behind the woman, then she spun and raised the shard above her head. She squeezed it tighter, wincing as it sliced deep into her palm. Blood streamed down her forearm, but she was already lunging at the stupefied woman, who had no time to react. She didn't take a single step backward or to the side. Instead, she held her arms out and leaned forward, assuming the crazed mass coming at her was someone in need of help.

For her intended good deed, the young woman received a deep slash across the face. Her left eye was destroyed at once. Her two lips became four. Blood flooded her throat, dampening her howls of pain. The maniac with the shard of glass pushed her down and straddled her. As the shard repeatedly rose and fell, it spit a faint, reddish reflection on the tile walls. The shard was buried in the shredded flesh of the woman's neck and then resurrected. After the woman's flailing arms fell limply to the ground, Irene continued to slash up her face until the skull was exposed.

Blood dripped from Irene's face and hair. Though the woman had stopped resisting, Irene kept stabbing until the shard broke in two—one piece lodged under the woman's collarbone and the other embedded in Irene's palm.

Out of breath, Irene staggered to her feet and looked down at herself. Her acid-wash jeans now looked more like crimson tie-dye. She held out her right hand, entranced by the blood streaming from her palm and spilling onto the dead woman below.

"Thank you," Irene said as she stepped over the body. And she meant it. She felt better than she had since leaving home.

Irene was bathed in blood, so she did not bother to wash it off. But she did return to the sink to take another sizable mirror fragment with her. Just in case she started to feel down again and needed to take it out on someone.

She left the restroom, got back into her car at pump number three, and drove off without a clue as to where she would go.

In the end, she wouldn't make it far.

She never got around to filling the gas tank.

WHAT THEY DON'T TELL YOU ABOUT HELL

"Give me another smoke, will ya?"

"Almost out."

"Have to make a stop."

"Getting pretty tired. Maybe we should, you know...give it up. Find someplace to zonk out."

The driver peered sideways at his companion. "What? You gonna turn chickenshit on me now? You said you was into wild shit. Having a good time. Gettin' your rocks off. Well, are ya or ain'tcha?"

"Yeah, man. I am. But, I mean, what do you plan to do anyway? You said you would take me south, but we've been heading west for three hours already. If you don't plan on heading to Florida anymore, it's no problem, man. Alright? Just let me out someplace where I can get a hot meal. I'll grab another ride when I can."

"Relax. Just a little detour. Take care of business, and then south it is. We'll cut right through the goddamn Smoky Mountains. You really think I could say no to all that fine beach pussy? Fuck me...Daytona, here I come." Thrusting his hips, he pantomimed jerking himself off and climaxing on the steering wheel. The car did a couple swift daredevil swerves, nearly swiping the side mirror of an oncoming Honda.

The passenger, Benito Gomez, gripped the dashboard and held his breath. When the car was cruising steadily in the lane again, he let out a nervous laugh, trying not to look at the driver. Benito had left Rochester five days earlier. Hitchhiking had been more difficult than he thought. He'd only been picked up once in the first two days, and the old man had been local, so he hardly covered three miles. The next few days were better. Between six different drivers, he managed to make it farther south but found it challenging to get to the coast. A zigzagging course finally deposited him in Pittsburgh, where he took a rest day in a cheap motel. All those drivers had been regular folks, friendly but not too talkative.

This driver, who had given three different names so far, was like a stick of dynamite. He claimed to be headed for Florida himself and was more than willing to take Benito all the way. But after a piss break outside Uniontown, he said he had something to take care of first—"Just a quick detour"— and proceeded to head west. It took about an hour for Benito to realize what the guy had in mind.

"Forget about that. Florida it is. Promise. I just need to... I really need to get this outta my system first. That the last cig?"

Benito lit his smoke, crumpled the pack, and tossed it out the window. "Last one."

"You got money?"

"A little. Enough for smokes and a meal a day until I get to Fort Lauderdale. Just stop at the next chance, and I'll get a new pack. I can get one for you, too."

The driver grinned and shook his head. "Not much of a smoker. Only when I can bum them. Good way to keep bad habits in check."

"I hear ya."

They continued in silence for a while. The driver seemed to

become restless, accelerating at a slow but steady pace until they caught up to the Taurus. For a moment, Benito thought the guy might pull up alongside it again. Suddenly, he let off the gas. As the car fell back, the driver started humming.

After a while, the driver said, "So, what's in Fort Lauderdale?"

"Family," answered Benito, flicking the cigarette butt out the window. "Well, my grandmother. My brother's down in Miami, in prison."

"For what?"

"I don't even know this time. Assault, drugs, rape? Who knows? He's been in and out since we were teenagers."

"Grandma know you're coming?"

"Yes and no, I guess. I didn't call and tell her, but...she warned me not to go to New York. She knew I'd fuck up. Get in trouble, go broke, live on the streets. Just like my old man. She knew it, and she was right. So, I guess she's probably expecting me. What about you?"

The driver shrugged. "Never been, but always wanted to. Shit, I've never been out of the Northeast. Farthest I ever got was...well, right now, I suppose. Never been as far as Ohio. Been to hell, but not Ohio and sure as shit not Florida."

Benito laughed, but when he glanced at the driver, he saw pain in the man's expression and shut his mouth. "Shit, man. Sorry, I didn't mean to... You're serious, aren't you?"

"'Fraid so."

"Wish I had some more smokes."

"Gotta be a gas station coming up. Been a while since the last one."

"But I thought you wanted to...you know?"

"Ah, she ain't gonna get far. I'll fill up. You hurry on inside and grab your smokes. Maybe a bottle of hooch, too, if they're selling this late."

Benito gazed out the window.

"You wanna know, don't you?" said the driver.

"Wanna know what?"

"What hell's like."

Still staring out the window, Benito fought with himself. Something had happened to this crazy fuck, and goddamn right he wanted to know. But his gut was telling him to say no. Hell was a bad place. He'd been damn close himself, and now he was running back to Grandma's protective bosom because he hadn't liked it too much. Who would?

"Sure…"

"So, about a year ago," the driver starts at once, "I'm at the local dive with a couple of buddies from high school. We used to get together every two weeks or so at one of the bars around town—"

"Where?"

"Portland."

"I thought you'd never been west of Ohio."

"Portland, Maine, dipshit. Anyhow, we're at the bar, and I'm checkin' out this chick and her friend all night. Just before last call, my buddies start headin' out, but these chicks are still there, so I hang back, waitin' to see if, you know, if they need a ride or anything. So I order one more and just hawk over them. They've been there almost as long as I have, drinking cocktails and taking shots. They're lit up, just like me, right? So I'm thinkin', piece of cake. Play my cards right and I may even talk them into a threesome. Then, just as I'm about to make a move, this old guy slithers out of a booth in the back, walks right up to them, and sits down at their table. They play along at first, but I can tell they're startin' to get the heebie-jeebies. So I finish my beer and go over to tell the old guy to fuck off. He doesn't say anything but just stares at me for a long time and finally leaves without a word. Then—can you believe this?— these bitches tell me to fuck off! Well, I get pissed and make a few…rude remarks. Call them dirty names and cuss them out until the bartender grabs me by the collar and throws me right the fuck outta there. And guess who's waitin' outside?"

Benito realized the driver actually wanted him to answer. He shrugged and said, "The old guy?"

"Bingo! He's standing right by the door, leerin' and grinnin' at me. I get in his face and shout at him a bit, but I'm so shit-faced I'm probably not makin' any sense, just mindless obscenities. I hop into my car and head for home. But this motherfucker, he follows me. Like I said, I'm so blitzed that I'm barely able to keep 'er steady in the lane, so I never notice the headlights shining up my ass. But he follows me back to my apartment and pulls in right behind me. When I get out and realize it's the same fuckin' wackjob from the bar, I see red. But he comes at me with somethin' in his hand and whacks me one. Just like in the movies, man. Night-night. When I wake up, I don't know where I am, but I don't like the looks of it. It's dark, dingy, moist. It smells like sweat and paint thinner. Rust and mildew. Piss and rat shit. Jesus Christ..."

The driver paused to swallow. He leaned his head out the window for a blast of fresh air and hocked a thick bolt of phlegm.

"Doesn't take me long to realize I'm in some kind of fuckin' torture chamber. The cinder block walls tell me it's a basement, but I'm restrained and not going anywhere fast. Believe you me, I tried. Ain't until he comes down to feed me that I get some light and can get a lay of the land. The blood, man. I throw up and can't eat a thing, even though he's trying to force-feed me some kind of tasteless gruel or porridge or some shit. Uh-uh, it just comes right back up. The blood is every-where. I mean it—*everywhere*. Most of it's old and dried, but some looks thick and, like, congealed. And it isn't just like someone bled out in a puddle. It had been sprayed on every wall, plastered in every crevice. I notice stains on the rafters and on every old piece of junk down there. Against one wall, there's this shelf filled with all kinds of normal shit, you know, paint cans, duct tape, wood scraps, sleeping bags, whatever. One row holds what I first think are tools for woodworking or something. But they aren't tools. Not regular tools. They're fuckin' torture devices. Look homemade, you know? Like, crafted with care and attention to detail. And there are bones, too. Human bones. Just scattered around the ground like they've been forgotten. Scraps of flesh and hair. Goddamn. Every time he comes down, I keep telling him to just kill me already. Just get it over with, but he won't do it, and I'm starting to lose it. Already lost the will to live, and now my mind is going, too. Then, one day—I'd probably been there a week or so—he brings down another victim. No bullshit— couldn't if I wanted, not on my mother's life—it's that same fuckin' broad from the bar. I recognize her immediately, and the old guy knows I do. He grins like it's exactly what he wants."

Benito had begun to breathe heavier. He tried to keep his eyes trained straight ahead but couldn't help glancing at the driver. He needed to figure out whether the guy was telling the truth. Something about the feverish way he told the story made it sound like he enjoyed it, and Benito wondered whether he'd hopped a ride with an honest-to-God psychopath.

"I really need another smoke..." Benito muttered, hoping to distract the driver from continuing.

"Yeah, yeah. Look there, up ahead. See those lights. That'll be a Shell or a Mobile or somethin'. Has to be. You get your smokes, grab us a bottle of snake juice, and I'll fill up. Then, we catch up to this bitch."

"We can't just keep going in the wrong direction. If you wanna go after her, I can't stop you. But I really need to get to Florida, man. Just let me out so I can flag down another driver, alright?"

"No can do. I need your help."

"What do you need to catch up to her so badly for, man? You'll probably just freak her out anyway. What'll you do? Ask her out on a date? Ask her to come to Florida? You're not gonna rape her."

The driver leers at Benito and gives a sly grin. "Gonna do a helluva lot more than that."

"Wha—" Benito choked on his own saliva.

"Let me tell you what I wanna do to her. Hell is a bad place, my friend. A bad place... But what no one ever tells you about hell is that it gets into you. Weasels right into your soul like a virus. Sure does. It lives inside you, and slowly but surely...it changes you."

"What do you mean?"

"The guy brings this woman down the stairs and throws her to the ground right in front of me, right? Her face is already bruised and cut up. She sees me, and I see it. I see it..."

"See what?"

"She recognizes me, too. Then she notices the chains securing me to the post. She sees the blood and smells my filth. The horror in her eyes is... I never seen anything like it. It's like a mirror, a monster, and a precious memory all rolled into one. And he tells me what he's gonna do. She's sprawled right there at his feet, listenin', shiverin', whimperin' as he describes it in hideous detail. And then he does it. He rapes her right in front of me, beatin' her with somethin' that looks like a belt, but it's studded. And goddamn if he isn't starin' at me! Grinnin' at me the entire time. Over her screams, he's shoutin' at me, '*You're next! You're next, you dumb fuck! Gonna make it worse for you! Long and slow! Gonna take my time!*' And you know what?"

"Wait—this can't be real. You're telling me some kind of campfire story."

"You think I'm a fuckin' liar?" growled the driver. He let off the gas and glared at Benito.

"No, man! No, that's not what I meant. Just, but... seriously?"

"You're lookin' at a man who's been to hell, amigo. Been to hell and brought it back with him..."

"But then...how'd you get out of there?"

With a smirk, the driver stepped on the gas again and pointed ahead. "See? What'd I tell you? Good ol' Exxon, just when we need one." He slowed and pulled into the empty lot.

"What about her?" Benito indicated the car they'd been following as its tail lights faded into the night. "Probably time to let her go now, huh? Head south. To Florida."

"We'll catch up to her. We've got to because..." He parked next to one of the pumps and shut off the engine. "You never let me finish. You know what I felt when that maniac was workin' on her, not three feet in front of me, her blood spraying onto my fuckin' face with each blow and her screams rippin' holes in my eardrums? You know what I felt? Total bodily euphoria. Better than the cleanest Horse. My mind emptied completely. No more fear. The tempting pleasures of hell won me over. I got an erection like a goddamn redwood and instantly blew my load. I wanted it. I wanted to watch him. I wanted to be him. So you hurry up inside, chief. Go get your smokes so we can catch up to this piece of ass. It's been a year already...and I've been jonesin' to relive the best goddamn night of my life."

Benito went pale. He made no move to open the door.

"Hey! I said hurry up, fuckwad! And if you try to run or alert anyone, I'll do you in before I go and get her. I'll fuck her on top of your corpse."

Walking inside, Benito told himself he would get the clerk to call the cops and lock the doors. He would explain that they had to keep the deranged nutjob at pump one locked outside. But he was hardly able to think. He forgot all about any kind of bottle, barely mumbled the word "smokes," and just took the

Marb Reds the guy gave him without complaint, even though he always smoked lighter cigarettes. Sweat poured down his forehead, shudders ran up and down his spine, and his legs felt too weak to hold him up. On his way out, he thought maybe he ought to slip off into the darkness without saying a word and head in the other direction on foot. But the guy was glaring at the door and waiting for him. Numb terror hooked Benito and reeled him right back into the LeSabre's passenger seat. The entire stop took less than two minutes.

The driver squealed out of the gas station, fishtailing onto the road and still heading west. He had the accelerator punched to the floor, staring out the windshield with crazed, greedy eyes.

"What's your name again, man?" asked Benito.

"Travis Sterling," answered the driver absently. "We're gonna catch her, I guarantee it..."

"Then what happened? I mean, how'd you—"

"His kid."

"His kid what?"

"Not a kid. His son. Grown man. Older'n you, younger'n me. Maybe. Hard to tell how old he was because he seemed kinda slow. Good guy, but not all there mentally. Like, stunted. Makes sense since his pa was a homicidal maniac. Sure must've seen some shit, you know? You must've seen it on the news. What happened was, after the old guy finishes with the girl, he leaves her dead body lying right on my feet. She's spread across my shins, and her blood is soakin' into my jeans, my socks. Now that it's my turn, my, uh...gratification is crashing hard and fast, right? As I watch him go and select his next tool—the one he's gonna use on me—I can see my death. I can already feel it, right? Outta nowhere, someone breaks down the fuckin' door, runs down the stairs three or four at a time, and comes at the old man with a gigantic fuckin' pair of scissors. They struggle a bit, but the young guy lands a good blow with the blade, so the old man is losin' blood real fast. The whole time, the kid is cryin' and wailin', Daddy-this and Daddy-that. He's so bent out of shape that he barely notices me. He sees the dead woman lyin' across my legs and even tries to kick her outta the way, but it's like he's lookin' right through me or something. So me, I start thinkin' I might be dead already. The light in the old man's eyes is long gone by now, but the son keeps chopping at him with these scissors. Finally, I'm the one screaming, and the kid finally looks at me. Turns out I was covered in so much blood he thought I was dead. Now, he knows I'm not, so he unchains me and tells me to wait in that fuckin' dungeon, that he'll be right back. He runs upstairs and comes back a minute later with a pistol. Unloads the thing on his pa's lifeless body. Then, we ran. Together. The least I could do was help him get away with it. Got us cleaned up, then started hitching, just like you. Turned out we were just outside Boston, in the fuckin' suburbs. That's where he did his work, but he took his victims from all over New England. It didn't feel right goin' back to Portland, so I took the kid and brought him to New York. Then...he ditched me." The driver paused, chuckling nostalgically, and added, "That fuckin' nut saved my life. Only not in time. A little bit of hell got into the both of us."

"Look, maybe, uh...Travis, right?" Benito's hand is already on the door handle, but Travis is still accelerating. They must be doing almost ninety. "Maybe we just leave this poor girl alone, yeah? What do you say? Let's just go to Florida. Seems like both of us need a fresh start. You'll love the sunshine, man. Makes you feel alive. Brand new. And the ocean down there, it can wash everything away. Alright? I'm serious. You don't need to—"

"Shut the fuck up. It's too late. For both of us. The Tinker-mans ruined my life. That old man opened a wound in my soul and poured his putrid evil into it. He made me like it. What he did...what I saw...now, I only want more. I've been keepin' it in check for more'n a year, but I can't no more. And his goddamn son... Goddamnit, Steve, why didn't you just let him kill me? Instead, he let him infect me, and then he just turned me loose. Now...now I have to..."

Neither noticed how quickly they came upon the woman's car. Travis had to slam on the brakes because he never realized the Taurus wasn't moving. It was parked in the lane with the driver's side door hanging open. Though he was scared stiff, even Benito recognized the odd circumstances and felt a little jolt, a surge of interest, a mystery to be solved.

Both Travis and Benito got out of the car. Travis pulled a gun out from under his seat. Benito hesitated but didn't think he had a choice. He did not doubt that Travis would shoot him if he tried to get in his way with the girl.

The woman's car was empty, to which Benito mumbled a silent prayer of gratitude, only to trail off when he glanced up at the front bumper. Something was floating in front of the vehicle. It hung in the air, two or three feet off the ground, and appeared to be rising higher. The headlights illuminated it bright and clear, so there was no question what it was. But how?

"The fuck?" said Travis, coming up along the driver's side. "Is that what I think it is?"

"Yeah," answered Benito from the passenger side.

"She hit him and made a run for it... Sneaky fuckin' bitch..."

"I don't think that's what we should be worried about. Don't you see?"

"What? She can't be far. Just hiding in the field here. We'll find—"

"Travis, don't you see that?"

"Just some dead Chinaman."

"He's floating in mid-air! Something's wrong here!"

"You're telling me somethin's wrong. This bitch isn't getting away on my watch."

"No, I mean...don't you feel that. We're not alone."

"Because she's hiding right there in the fuckin' field! I'm telling you—"

"Not her. Something else..."

As Benito watched the Asian man with the mutilated face move higher into the air, his eyes drifted upward, and he realized the sky was gone. No, not gone exactly, but blocked out by something even darker. It wasn't a cloud or anything fantastical either, like a giant winged monster or a UFO. It was an elemental darkness. The black of dreams and the afterlife. The endless compression of a black hole. An awful, haunting nothingness.

"Where the fuck did she go?" growled Travis.

"Where do you think? She just killed someone! And—"

"Good. Then we won't have to feel bad for what we're about to do to her."

"But how do you explain this? Is there something wrong with my eyes? That dead guy's floating, right? Right?"

"I don't give a shit about the dead Chinaman. I want the girl. Find her."

"How's it possible? She must be toying with us. I told you she saw us..."

"So what if the bitch saw us? What's she gonna do?"

"Don't you see this shit? That guy's flying! She's not a bitch, she's a fucking witch! Come on, Travis. I think we gotta get outta here—"

"Shut up, you spineless immigrant shit! Listen! Did you hear that?"

"Hear what?"

"There. Shh."

Travis pointed into the field to their left, but Benito kept staring at the body. It was not floating; something within the blackness seemed to be lifting it up, pulling or sucking it in. Then, a shape emerged. A long, wispy limb extended from it, grabbing the scraped and battered dead man and lifting the body higher until it floated maybe twenty feet in the air.

"Look!" Benito pointed above.

Travis jumped at the sound of his voice. He scowled across the hood, and when he saw Benito's hand pointing, he raised his gun.

Two indistinct creatures moved inside the darkness. They were not large and seemed almost fragmentary, like coils of smoke in a breeze. When Travis fired a shot, they instantly became agitated and merged into one, wavering and swimming through the hovering black pit. The entire black mass began to ripple and emit a low hum. No longer were there two manageable creatures but a single colossal beast. It dropped out of the blackness into the center of the road, though it still towered above them.

Whatever it was, it did not seem biologically or geometrically possible. It did, however, seem angry. Perhaps anger was the wrong word. Travis unloaded his weapon at the unnameable atrocity, and Benito remembered Travis's explanation of how he felt in that basement—repulsion, terror, and bliss all at the same time. Those were the emotions Benito sensed from the creature as it bit into Travis's gun-wielding arm and tore it off with hardly any effort. Benito could not make out the creature's reactions—he could not even identify a face—but its fervor radiated in a pulsing wave. It reminded Benito of bass thumping from enormous subwoofers or heat waves rising off the concrete in a South Florida summer.

The shadowy monster stabbed some sort of appendage through Travis's chest to stabilize him while it wrenched off the rest of his limbs. It kept him alive, saving his head for last in what seemed like a mocking form of torment, and then launched his limbless, headless torso into the air. Benito saw it splat and bounce, probably thirty yards away, staining the yellow dashes in the center of the road.

Benito looked in the woman's car. The keys were still in the ignition, and the engine was running, but it was pinched between Travis's Buick and the suspended dead body, which the creature had lowered during the attack. The Buick was still running, too, so Benito turned on his heels, running faster than he ever had before, and he had run from the cops on plenty of occasions. Sometimes the cops caught him, and sometimes they didn't. He thought of his grandma and prayed that luck was on his side tonight.

He swerved past the hood, leaping around the open door and diving into the driver's seat. A colossal strength followed him into the car and coiled around his waist. Squirming violently, he saw a long, disjointed tentacle stretched out from some indefinable part of the creature. Just like the floating body, it hoisted him off the ground. Lifting Benito high and fast, it swung him in a high arc that reached a pinnacle of a hundred feet before bringing his head down onto the asphalt like an ax.

In the moments before he died, Benito believed he heard two voices emitting cries of vengeance, satiation, and ecstasy.

GOAT STEW

Yu-mi Lee tightened her grip on the rope. The goat bucked and kicked, screeching with preternatural fright. Anyone who claimed animals were ignorant creatures had clearly never killed one before. As the animal struggled, Yu-mi thought she would lose her hold on the rope. In her other hand, she held her phone, aiming the screen at the goat. She tried to entice it to look, both to distract it from its imminent demise and to instill the woman's image in its mind.

Her aunt, Myung-sook Park, chanted a haunting lament, growing more insistent and forceful as she approached. Her voice drove the goat into a frenzy. Nearby, the rest of the animals grew agitated in their pens. The chicken coop shook and rattled. The hogs squealed and the dogs howled. Molly the horse snorted and stomped. At the far end of Myung-sook's property, the sheep and goats bleated fearfully into the night.

Yu-mi bent her knees, squeezed the rope tighter, and adjusted her phone.

"Will you tell my mom to hurry up?" a man's voice blared from the earpiece. "People are starting to look at me funny."

Though Yu-mi felt the same way, she could not respond.

She had muted the phone on her end to make sure nothing was heard on his end. Briefly, she tilted the screen to check that he still had the woman in the frame. He did. The woman was still sitting on the park bench, smiling at folks as they walked past. She had a book in her lap and kept raising a large reusable tumbler to her mouth.

"*I-mo*, how long will this ta—"

"Hush, Yu-mi! Don't interrupt!" Myung-sook hissed without looking at her niece. She shook off the interruption and resumed her chanting even louder than before. Grabbing hold of the horns, she squatted onto her haunches and shoved her forehead into the goat's face. The animal screeched, and Myung-sook answered with a savage wail of her own. She took the phone from Yu-mi and showed it to the animal, forcing it to see the woman on the screen. She wrapped her arm around the goat's neck, soothing it, lowering her chant to a consistent, calming whisper.

After two minutes, Myung-sook had worked the goat into a kind of trance. She nodded to Yu-mi and handed the phone back to her. Then, she stepped over to the small table holding her wares, including the stack of hanji sheets upon which they had written out Chinese characters defining the bounds of the curse. One by one, she lifted them, uttering the word scrawled upon each. She rolled the stack tightly and held it over the fire, igniting the tip like a torch. Holding it out, she stepped up to the goat and pressed it against the animal's flank.

The goat leaped and attempted to run. Yu-mi stared in sick fascination. The sudden jerking movement tore her shoulder out of its socket. She winced and groaned, stretching as she tried to pop it back into place.

Without breaking the rhythm of her chants, Myung-sook turned a meaningful glare on Yu-mi, informing her to hold on tight. At this point, Yu-mi no longer understood most of the words her aunt spoke, but she felt confident this was the curse itself being spoken.

After burning two Chinese characters into the goat's side, Myung-sook pressed the nub of burning paper into the goat's forehead, momentarily stunning it. Yu-mi whimpered and turned away, but her eyes wandered back to the scorched fur on the goat's forehead. When she had first approached her aunt about placing a curse on the woman, she never thought she would have to be here for it. She felt sick to her stomach yet could not take her eyes off the surreal ritual.

Yu-mi never even saw Myung-sook grab the machete from the table. All she saw was a flash as the blade swept down, light from the fire reflecting off the pristine steel. A stream of blood sprayed her face and robe. The goat's head hit the ground, tumbling and wobbling before coming to rest with its eyes open and—possibly the creepiest part of the entire sacrifice—still staring directly at the woman on Yu-mi's phone screen.

The machete clattered to the ground. Myung-sook followed, crumpling to her knees and then falling onto her side. Her eyes rolled back in her head. Minor convulsions coursed through her limbs.

Yu-mi had seen this happen at the end of past rituals, though always from the periphery. She had never been so close before. Never been involved. Quickly, she dropped the rope and unmuted her phone. A red smear streaked the screen.

"Kang-min, what do I do? What do I do? Your mom fell over! You know, how she does at the end! Is she seizing? Is she okay? Should I do something?"

"Finally. Do you have any idea what kind of stares I'm getting around here? I'm pretty sure she noticed me filming her, by the way—"

"Shut up, Kang-min! Tell me what to do!"

"I don't know, Cousin! Just relax, for one. I told you, I never wanted anything to do with my mom's creepy shaman shit, alright. That's why I stayed here after college, so I wouldn't have to be near it anymore. It's always scared the hell out of me. Even from another country, you still managed to rope me into it. I'm not too fucking happy about this."

"Yeah, well, you fucking owe me. Maybe you shouldn't have done that sick shit to me as a teenager. For such a perverted fuck, you're getting off light, as far as I'm concerned."

"Fuck, Yu-mi. How many times do I have to tell you I'm sorry?"

"You're not sorry. You never apologized until I fucking blackmailed you."

"Goddamnit. Is she still...seizing?"

"I think she's coming to. No thanks to you."

"Yeah, you're welcome. I didn't have to do this, you know. And I'd better see that money in my account before Friday."

"Can you still see her? Has anything happened yet? Is it working?"

"Fuck no, I got the hell out of there. It was only a matter of seconds before the cops showed up to ask questions. And you know it takes longer than two minutes for a curse to start working, right?"

"*I-mo? I-mo?* Are you okay? Fuck, Kang-min, she's not— *Aahhhh!*"

"What? Yu-mi, what? What happened?"

"It moved! It fucking moved!"

"What did?"

"The fucking goat's head!"

"Oh fuck this..." said Kang-min, lifting a trembling finger to disconnect the call.

. . .

After Myung-sook built the bonfire, she took Yu-mi's cotton robe and held it up, showing her niece the startling red pattern splattered across the front. As the blood drained from the goat's neck, Yu-mi had been standing right in the puddle, so the bottom of her robe had soaked it up. The entire bottom hem was stained a deep burgundy.

Myung-sook held it out, offering it to Yu-mi, who held up her hands and backed away.

"Are you sure?" asked her aunt. "A souvenir to remember your introduction to our arts?"

Yu-mi looked away, shaking her head. "I don't want to be reminded, *I-mo*. I just...I think I'm going to be sick..."

With a shrug, Myung-sook turned away. "That's how we all start, dear. But you'll be back. Next time, to learn. After you see the results—what you have brought about—you'll be back. It's the only way."

"The only way for what?"

Myung-sook sighed as she balled up the robe and tossed it onto the fire. The flames receded beneath its weight before slowly consuming it.

"These things we do, they are not isolated," Myung-sook said. "What we have done tonight will have far-reaching effects. It's already a part of something bigger than you realize. *You* are a part of it, Yu-mi. Have no doubt—it will work. It has already worked. You will see the results before long. And feel them. That woman—whoever she is—she will suffer. The power you feel will become an elixir to heal all ailments. But you will also find that you, yourself, and those around you are not exempt from the influence of our art. This act will cling to you whether you keep the evidence or not. It attaches to your spirit and will continue to affect the world around you. There is only one way to keep it in check."

"How?" Yu-mi asked tentatively.

Myung-sook looked at her niece with a smirk, raising her

eyebrows suggestively. "You continue down this path. Always offering more."

"What if I don't?"

"It is not for everyone. You must not feel...obligated. Insincerity begets its own curses."

"*I-mo?*"

"Yes?"

"If I don't offer more?"

Myung-sook smiled weakly and sighed. "You don't want to know."

Yu-mi's legs felt weak, ready to give way. She stumbled over to a log stool and sat down. Her breaths became heavier as she stared at the flames, inhaling the thick smoke from the smoldering robe. "I-mo, how many times have you done this?"

"More than I could count, dear." Myung-sook walked over to Yu-mi, resting her hands on her niece's shoulders. "I was younger than you when I started. A jilted lover, pregnant with Kang-min by a man who left the moment he found out. I sought help from a reclusive shaman who lived in the mountains near my village. Most of the villagers believed she was a ghost, but she was real, and she was powerful. She helped me get revenge on that shit of a man, and I swore I would never return to her. But she only laughed and told me the same thing I'm telling you now."

Shaking her head, Yu-mi pulled her shoulders away from her aunt's grasp and stood up. She backed away, on the verge of hyperventilating. "This was wrong. I think I made a mistake. That girl, she didn't even... Neither did Rick... It's just me being a shitty, jealous wife..."

"Relax, dear. It's too late for that. I asked you to consider these things before we started. Now, what's done is done. Listen to me—regret only makes it worse. Do you understand?"

Yu-mi sniffled and wiped her eyes. As she nodded at her

aunt, her gaze fell upon the goat's headless body. The bloody pool slowly drained off the slanted slab through the drainage hole. Thankfully, the head was turned away. Yu-mi was still freaked out by what she thought she saw after it was chopped off—a sneer, a blink, a wagging tongue.

"I must clean up back here," said Myung-sook, "before the flies. You can help if you'd like, but I don't recommend it in your state."

"What do you...do with it?"

"First, I'll have to dismember it. The head goes on the altar and remains there for four days, until the maggots rise. The limbs and hide, into the fire. The entrails will make a fine treat for my menagerie. And the rest, I'll boil in a stew that will feed us for a week."

"I think I'd better..."

"Yes, you should go inside and get washed up. We can talk more when I'm finished here."

"No, I think I should leave. I should go back to Rick."

"Yu-mi, it's the middle of the night. The first train won't leave for hours. And you should allow your mind some time to process what you've experienced tonight. You will not be the same after—"

"I'm sorry, *I-mo*. Thank you, but I can't...I can't stay here..."

With a disappointed sigh, Myung-sook nodded. She had hoped her niece would be a quick convert, attracted by the feverish atmosphere of the ritual. Squatting down, Myung-sook picked up the goat's head. She tilted it to look into its eyes before glancing at Yu-mi. "It's not a good idea, but I can see that your mind is made up. So, go. The guest room will be prepared if you change your mind."

Yu-mi hurried away, following the stone path back to the house. A moment later, Myung-sook heard the rear door slide open and shut. Within five minutes—while she was hacking off the goat's limbs—she heard a taxi pull up and honk its horn out front.

"What do you think?" Myung-sook said to the dead-eyed goat. "Did she even bother to wash the blood from her hands and face? The stains on her shoes? Surely, she still stinks of death. She'll learn soon enough that people can tell."

The four goat legs smoked on the fire, filling the air with the scent of burning hair and flesh. On the altar, the head sat mounted on a weighted stone spike. Blood had pooled beneath it and was dripping off the table. The animal's empty eyes and lolling mouth kept watch as Myung-sook carved into the body. She shoved her hands inside and methodically ripped out the organs, setting them aside on the slanted concrete platform.

After making the final cut to the hide, Myung-sook set down the knife and grunted as she tore the skin away from the body. Panting, she stood and held it up, admiring her work. A trail of blood followed her over to the fire pit. She shoved the hide into the coals, briefly subduing the flames before it caught on the hair and fat, flaring up wildly. Nearby, the dogs growled. A disturbance sounded in the chicken coop.

Off to the side of the platform, Myung-sook plunged her arms into the rain barrel. She scrubbed the gore from her hands and forearms, taking care to scrape underneath her fingernails. In the stable, Molly let loose a series of wild snorts. The wood creaked as though the horse had leaned her weight against it.

Myung-sook filled the bucket from the barrel and threw the water onto the platform, watching as the blood washed down the incline onto the gravel below. She repeated this several times. Something whisked past overhead, most likely a bat. The sheep bleated manically, working the goats into a panic.

The animals often reacted severely to her sacrifices. This had always been one of her least favorite things about performing this particular ritual. The animals would be jumpy and rowdy for a day or two, then return to normal. After thirty years of this, she had grown used to it, but the noise would make it hard to sleep. And if Yu-mi returned, as Myung-sook assumed she would, she would almost certainly spend a sleepless night listening to the animal's haunting choir.

For a while, Myung-sook stood near the fire. She held out her hands, absorbing the warmth as she watched the flesh melt off the dismembered legs. The hide became a smoldering mess of charred hair and bubbling fat. Over the years, the sickly sweet scent of burning blood had become intoxicating to her.

Suddenly, the dogs went wild. They barked with an unhinged fervor she had only heard once before—during her childhood when black bears still roamed the mountains near the village where she grew up. She knew why they were barking and didn't bother to shush them. Better to let them get it out of their system.

Just as suddenly as they started, they stopped. It wasn't only the dogs that went silent, but all the animals. Myung-sook heard nothing but the crackling of the fire. In the nearby woods, the brush rustled violently like someone was trampling through it. Then, behind her, something fell with a heavy thud.

Myung-sook jumped and pressed her hand to her chest. Her heart galloped as she turned around, hoping to find that Yu-mi had changed her mind and returned already.

The goat's head had tumbled to the ground. It lay on its side below the altar, the dirt darkening beneath it as blood leaked from the severed neck and from the mouth.

Exhaling a deep breath, Myung-sook gathered the long folds of her cotton robe in her hands and approached the altar. She picked up the head by the horns, glancing at the altar and wondering how it fell. The altar was perfectly level, the legs were balanced, and the stone spike she displayed the head on had not tipped over.

Still gripping the horns, she scrutinized the altar's integrity when the goat's teeth clacked together. Bewildered, she glanced down and saw it blink. The hazy lifelessness that had recently found a home in its eyes vanished, replaced by an intelligent glimmer.

With a short, stunted scream, Myung-sook prepared to fling the head away.

"Do not do that. You will only make it worse." The goat's mouth moved, leaving no question as to where the deep, breathy, taunting voice originated.

Myung-sook screamed again, this time louder, longer.

"That is fine. Scream all you want. Your nearest neighbors live beyond the surrounding hills. Your niece is gone. You were correct; she will be back to discover you. And to get a taste of the fate that awaits her."

"Wh-what is this?" Myung-sook stuttered. "What do you want? I have kept my oaths. I have not stepped beyond my... my... Please! What do you want? What can I do? I'll do anything!"

The bodiless head laughed derisively. Soon, all the animals joined in, creating a disorienting chorus of laughter. Holding the head out at arm's length, Myung-sook spun around. She could not see the other animals through the darkness, but their chaotic, intermingled cackles clawed at her ears.

As she spun, she noticed movement in the fire pit. The four legs righted themselves, rocking back and forth as the hooves found their footing atop the pile of burning wood. Moving together, as though they were still attached to a body, they pranced out of the flames and over to the concrete platform where the animal's fleshless, hollow trunk lay. The hooves hopped up in unison, then knelt down and worked together to wedge beneath the lump of bloody muscle and bone. Tilting from side to side, the four legs balanced the body between them, adjusting to orient it more or less naturally. Blood spilled out from the hollow trunk as the charred, smoking legs wobbled toward Myung-sook.

They stopped directly before her, nudging forward, pushing the bloodied stump of a neck into her belly, compelling her to place the head back where it belonged. She shook her head in resistance.

"Do not worry. I will not hurt you. I will be your salvation. You will pray to me as you always have."

"I can't...I can't..." Myung-sook blubbered.

"You have acted beyond your sphere, shaman," replied the goat, blood dribbling from its mouth. "A curse is laid without cause. It will spread because you have failed to heed our laws. You carried out this act without knowing what you were getting into. Never enter a forest without knowledge of the trails. Never enter a cave without a light to guide you. Your oath is void, Park Myung-sook."

"B-But I d-did... I asked her everything... My niece, she is im-im-impulsive..."

"The blame lies with she who speaks the words, she who wields the blade. You are responsible for the suffering of the undeserving. Therefore, you may no longer exert the influence you have held. You may no longer practice the ancient arts. Every request and call to the spirits you have served in your years must now come back to you. None can answer but you, yourself. If you hope for any small respite, make me whole. Otherwise, I can do nothing to limit your suffering."

Crying and shaking uncontrollably, Myung-sook extended her arms to place the severed ends of the goat's neck back together.

At once, a deafening crash sounded behind her. She was so startled by the grotesque sight of the goat—remade like a model from different mismatched pieces—that she did not even turn around to see the source.

Had she turned, she would have seen the wall of the chicken coop falling away, the dogs and the pigs bursting through the gates of their pens, and Molly kicking down the stable door. All the sheep and goats were stampeding toward her from the far end of the property. Bats began swooping underneath the awning, dozens of the screeching, winged critters crisscrossing back and forth. Finally, the brush in the woods parted as several wild boars charged out, snorting and huffing, long strands of saliva trailing from their mouths.

The dogs reached Myung-sook first. They had always been loyal animals. She'd raised them since they were pups. A few of them were almost fifteen years old. They clamped their teeth into her arms and dug their claws into her back, dragging her to the ground.

Next came the pigs, biting at the muscles of her legs, and the chickens, pecking at her face. Bats swooped down from above, nipping at her nose and eyes. The sheep came for her, biting into her scalp and tearing out clumps of hair. Myung-sook howled in agony as the young goats rammed their nubs into her sides and stomped their hooves into her collarbone. When the wild boars approached, the rest of the animals backed away, intimidated by their low, growling grunts and massive tusks. They charged, piercing her deeply and excruciatingly before taking large bites from the soft flesh of her stomach. Myung-sook nearly fell unconscious from the pain, but the sharp, rotten odor of the boars' coarse hair ran up her nostrils like a drill, ensuring she remained awake and present until the end.

The boars would have continued gnawing until they cleared every last bit of flesh from her bones, but Molly the horse had been looming nearby. She stomped frenetically, nudging the boars out of the way. With a deafening squeal, she reared up, stretching her forelegs high and briefly dancing as Myung-sook stared up in wild-eyed terror. Molly dropped her front hooves squarely onto Myung-sook's chest, crushing every one of her ribs and collapsing her lungs.

As Myung-sook heaved for air, she was vaguely aware of the dogs biting into her robe and dragging her away. By clamping onto her wrists, they pulled her up onto the concrete platform. All the animals crowded around her, forming a circle and parting at the front for the marionette goat to step through. It mounted the slab, clopping slowly around her body. Standing over her, it stared into her eyes. When it opened its mouth, blood poured onto Myung-sook's face, mingling with her own.

"Just like your niece, I may not have told you everything, but I did not lie. This seems to be a favorite trick of your kind. Now, I shall carry out my promise, though this is better than you deserve."

The goat placed its horns over the mutilated woman. The charred hooves dug into the platform, leaning hard and pushing the meaty body forward. Its head angled downward into Myung-sook's chest as one horn pierced directly through her heart. The shaman's suffering came to an unceremonious end, but for many others, the misery was only beginning.

THE MORNING AFTER

The police arrived early Friday morning. The building's superintendent refused to let them into the lobby and seemed prepared to stick to his guns. The officers discussed ways to force entry while a rookie cop decided to buzz the apartment they had been called to check out. There appeared to be some confusion about which apartment that was, and while they were bickering, a resident came out for his morning jog.

"Hello, fellas. There a problem?" The man held the door open but stood in the doorway so the cops would have to answer him first.

"That's what we're here to find out, sir. I'm Officer Winston. Have you heard anything out of the ordinary this morning?"

"Kinda hard to say. I'm a heavy sleeper, you see. Although, a sound from next door did wake me up before my alarm clock. And now that I think of it, I also heard some strange noises late last night when I was watching TV. They came from next door, too, but the other next door. I mean, not the same apartment, but—"

"Apartment 303?"

"303...? No. Me and my girl, Dawn, we're in 402. The sounds I heard came from 401 and 403. Strange. It's not like them. They're usually pretty quiet. 303 is Mrs Cazares. Why? Did something happen?"

"That's what we're here to find out. Sir, would you mind?"

"What?"

Officer Winston nodded at the door.

"Oh, yeah, of course! Sorry about that."

As he let the officers into the lobby, the superintendent's door swung open. Mr Lorenzo stuck his head out, his eyes bloodshot and his hair sticking out to one side. He glared angrily at the officers crowding into the lobby.

"Goddamnit, Grafton. Why'd you have to go and let them in?" he grumbled before turning to the officers. "I already told you nosy pricks, ain't nothing happened here. All I need is for you to get rid of that goddamn transient living in the alley."

While Officer Lebowicz remained in the lobby to deal with Mr Lorenzo and question Ben Grafton, Officers Winston and Cropp went up the stairs. Noreen Spinks from 203 had phoned the police at half past six. She opened the door before Winston even finished knocking. With an infant in her arms, she stepped into the hall, leaving the door open to keep an eye on the rest of her kids inside.

Noreen explained how, for the past two weeks or so, Mrs Cazares in 303 had been having the most awful dreams and hollering up a storm in the night. Her screams had kept the entire building on edge, but last night, she hadn't screamed. Noreen hadn't realized it, of course, since the silence allowed her to sleep through the night for once. Her third child, four-year-old Davey, woke her up just after six o'clock to tell her he'd wet the bed. While she got him cleaned up, she learned that the accident had not occurred in his sleep. He had hardly slept all night, constantly awoken by sounds from above. The two older children, Belinda and Warren, confirmed this. They had been woken by the sounds, too, but they were more used to strange sounds at night, so they had fallen back to sleep without issue.

With the kids all half-awake, she put on cartoons and started making coffee when she heard the scream. Unlike the previous two weeks, it did not come from the apartment directly above. That was when she realized Mrs Cazares had not screamed in the night. That, along with the ominous thudding noises her children had heard, was enough to prompt a call to the police.

"So, let me get this straight, ma'am," said Officer Winston. "You called us over here because your neighbor *did not* scream last night?"

"That's right," said Noreen. "I'm worried something happened to her. She's always been clumsy. She might have fallen and hurt herself. That would explain the sounds that woke the kids."

"Why didn't you go and check on her yourself?" asked Officer Cropp.

Noreen hesitated, averting her eyes and shifting her baby, little Rose, to her other arm. "It's just that...well, Mrs Cazares has been having these sort of spook dreams. Hearing her describe them has got me all kerfuffled myself. So I was...too scared to go into the hall. Especially since the scream I *did* hear sounded like it came from an insane asylum."

"So there was a scream?" clarified Cropp.

"Yes."

"Any idea which apartment it came from?" asked Winston.

Brusquely, Noreen shook her head. She kissed Rose on the temple. "Somewhere upstairs, I think. It wasn't Mrs Cazares, though. It was even louder. Shrill and real high-pitched, but... I'm pretty sure it was a man."

Winston and Cropp thanked Mrs Spinks, then headed up to the third floor. They knocked on 303 but got no answer. Down in the lobby, they found Ben Grafton annoyed by having his morning jog delayed while Mr Lorenzo screamed at Officer Lebowicz about the bum in the alleyway. Winston pulled the superintendent away and demanded to be let into apartment 303. Cropp asked Ben Grafton if he'd heard a scream on his floor between 6:15 and 6:20.

Ben Grafton shrugged. "I was in the shower."

Cropp looked him up and down. "You shower before going for a run?"

"Yeah, I..." Grafton stammered, suddenly self-conscious and evasive. "And after."

"How about you put off your run until we have a better grasp on what's going on around here?"

"Why? Am I under suspicion?"

Cropp squinted at Grafton. The other two cops turned to assess the situation.

"We may need to ask you a few questions," Winston piped in as Mr Lorenzo finally emerged with the keys. "That's all."

Across the hall, the door to 102 cracked open and Freddy Moore's frazzled, unshaven face poked out. His eyes were still drooping with sleep. He grumbled something that none of the cops could understand.

"That's exactly what I told them, Freddy," barked Mr Lorenzo as he headed up the stairs. "If they don't wanna deal with the real problems when I call, why should we have to put up with their goddamn nosing around at the crack of dawn?"

Officers Winston and Lebowicz followed the superintendent up to the third floor. Ben Grafton tapped Officer Cropp on the shoulder.

"That isn't what the old man said. He asked if the milkman had come around yet."

"The milkman?" asked Cropp.

Grafton nodded. "Mr Moore's like a hundred years old. He gets confused sometimes, especially when he's tired. IT'S

OKAY MR MOORE! THE MILK WILL BE HERE IN A FEW HOURS! YOUR NEWSPAPER, TOO!"

The old man nodded and finally opened his eyes. He flinched when he saw the uniform standing beside Ben Grafton, then grumbled something that sounded decidedly like a curse before slinking back into his apartment.

"So? Can I go for my run now?"

Cropp sighed and nodded. "Make it a quick one. And come right back here in case I need to speak with you again."

On the third-floor landing, Mr Lorenzo slipped the key into Mrs Cazares's door only to realize it was unlocked. He seemed unsettled by this and told the cops as much as he held the door open for them. Winston and Lebowicz shared a wary glance before entering. Just as they passed through the threshold, they jumped and froze, startled by a short screech from Mr Lorenzo. Cropp had crept up, spooking the superintendent from behind. None of them had heard him coming up the stairs.

With his hand resting on the butt of his weapon, Winston led the others into the apartment, calling out for a response from Carolynn Cazares. As he moved through the main living space, he pointed out a few overturned pieces of furniture and piles of collected junk, noting that someone must have rummaged through her things. From the doorway, Mr Lorenzo commented that her apartment was always a mess and had been ever since she moved in twenty-eight years ago.

Finding the bedroom door cracked open, Winston paused and glanced back. He pushed it open with his middle finger and immediately sucked a sharp breath through his teeth. Lebowicz and Cropp crowded in behind him, wincing as they poked their heads over his shoulder.

"What is it now?" growled Mr Lorenzo. "Better not be any damage to the goddamn room..."

Officer Lebowicz started to gag. Winston glared at him,

pushing him toward the kitchen and pointing at the super. "Get him out of here," he ordered.

Mrs Cazares's body lay sprawled face down on the floor beside her bed. The room was painted in blood. She appeared to have been stabbed dozens or even hundreds of times with a small blade. Her mattress was a literal pool of gore. Red splattered the walls, curtains, headboard, and even the ceiling. Slashes in the comforter and pillows revealed stuffing that looked like cherry-flavored cotton candy.

Other than a few items knocked off the nightstand, there didn't appear to be any other damage. Nothing had been ransacked in the bedroom or the rest of the apartment, suggesting this was not a robbery that got out of hand. Someone had entered the apartment with the sole purpose of butchering Carolynn Cazares.

Winston and Cropp got a real shock when they flipped over the body. Cropp went pale, and Winston did something he hadn't done since he was a teenager—he made the sign of the cross and muttered a quick prayer.

Not only did Mrs Cazares have just as many stab wounds on the front of her body as on the back, but her throat had been carved out. A fist-sized crater in her neck showed that the perpetrator had taken the time to carve through her windpipe and remove a handful of flesh. They could see the vertebrae at the back of her neck.

Fifteen minutes later, around the time more police arrived and started cordoning off the street, an ambulance arrived, insisting that they'd been called to this address. Officer Winston went out to inform them that they needed a hearse, not an ambulance, and also that they still had a hell of a lot to do before anyone touched the woman's body.

"Woman? We were called to pick up some lady's husband," answered the paramedic. "Apparently, he's having a severe panic attack or something. She thinks he might've cracked."

"Cracked? Which apartment?"

"403."

"You're going to have to hold on a... No, never mind. Come with me. I might need your help."

"Hey, we got a job to do too, pal—"

"Look, I've got a homicide in 303, and you just gave us our prime suspect."

Officer Winston brought the paramedics and a group of officers up to the fourth floor. Whitney Sweitzer answered the door, shocked to be met by three police officers with their guns drawn. She explained that her husband, Nathan Sweitzer, had become incommunicative and paranoid after several sleepless nights. Though she had slept through the night, she assured them that she had been woken constantly by Nate's restlessness. He'd been groaning and whimpering right until the sun came up. She insisted that there was no way he could have left the apartment without her knowing.

Soon, a detective named Art Knox arrived. He met with Nate and did a quick sweep of the Sweitzer apartment, determining that there was no way he could have murdered Mrs Cazares and gotten rid of every trace of blood. Whoever had killed her must have been drenched in it. Besides, they had yet to find the woman's throat, which meant the killer had most likely taken it with them. Just to be sure, he brought in a K-9 named Duey to sweep through the Sweitzer's place, and the dog found no missing body parts.

Detective Knox had already briefly spoken to several residents on the lower floors, from whom he had learned about Mrs Cazares's recent night screams. Henrick Lewiston in 301 seemed pleased that his neighbor's screams would no longer be a bother, showing no remorse over her death and demanding to know who the new screamer was. Knox pegged him as a suspect until another detail, repeated by several residents, struck him as significant. Aside from Mr Lewiston and the superintendent, all the other tenants had been worried about Mrs Cazares since the screaming started. Many of them had made a point of spending time with her and checking in regularly. They all reported the same thing about the recurrent nightmare she'd been having—she had been dreaming about her estranged daughter, Julieta, coming home to murder her as revenge for being a shitty mother.

Though Knox had never subscribed to investigative techniques that included dream theory and interpretation, he could not deny that this added a compelling element to the case. It seemed a hell of a lot more probable than a small-time offender like Henrick Lewiston risking life in the tank.

While the paramedics led Nate Sweitzer out, he panicked and refused to descend to the third-floor landing. He began screaming, a scream that several residents identified as the same scream they had heard that morning around 6:20. Waiting for the paramedics to sedate Mr Sweitzer, Detective Knox took the opportunity to speak with Dawn Ulmer in 402, who repeated the story about Mrs Cazares' nightmares. She claimed to have heard nothing in the night or that morning, as Mrs Cazares's screams forced her to start wearing noise-canceling headphones to bed. She also said her partner, Ben Grafton, may have heard something. However, since he was "an esteemed airhead," it probably went in one ear and out the other without him noticing. Knox thanked her and went to talk with the resident of 401.

The door was open.

He drew his weapon and nudged the door with his toe, calling into the apartment. When he received no response, he shouted down the stairwell for a few officers to back him up. The officers followed Knox inside, filtering through the two-room apartment with their weapons at the ready.

Detective Knox took the living room, where he discovered a man of Asian descent lying on the floor in a puddle of blood. A rusty Leatherman multi-tool was sticking out of his chest, jabbed directly into his heart. His arms and legs were splayed out, and he held his phone in his right hand. After prying it from the guy's fingers—already stiff with rigor mortis—Detective Knox found that the phone's auto-lock function had been disabled. When he swiped the screen, it opened to a messenger app with a recently received photograph and a short conversation in a foreign script.

Knox swore and took a deep breath, glancing from the gruesome photo to the young man on the floor.

"Looks like we got another one in here," he called to the officers searching the apartment. "You fellas finding anything?"

"Nothing, sir." The officers finished their sweep and joined Knox in the living room.

"Christ almighty," heaved Knox. "What the hell happened here last night? You see that..." He pointed at the Leatherman protruding from the man's chest. "Looks like the same type of blade that was used on the woman downstairs. And I don't know what the hell to think about this—"

When he showed the officers the photo on the man's phone, one ran into the hall, retching. It showed a middle-aged Asian woman lying on a concrete slab in the same position as the man—her limbs spread-eagled in a pool of carnage and an expression of utter horror petrified onto her face.

"What's that in her chest?" mumbled the remaining officer.

Knox ignored him and asked, "Any idea what language that is?"

"That's Korean. I had a fling with this girl who used to make me take her to the Korean barbecue places over in Flushing and—"

"Can you read it?"

"Hell no. Uh, I mean, no, sir."

"Shit. Alright, call this in. Tell them we've got another one. And find me someone who can read Korean."

Soon, another detective named Muney arrived. Knox walked Detective Muney through the building, explaining what he'd found and heard so far from the residents. They reconvened with Officer Winston in Mrs Cazares's kitchen, trying to wrap their heads around the ludicrous crime scene. They would have to seal off the entire building, find a place to take all the residents, and hope they came up with a lead on Julieta Cazares before she got too far. Detective Muney sent Winston to coordinate a team on 81st Street, asking the locals if they had seen or heard anything. Just after Winston left, a pair of men in suits poked their heads into the apartment.

"Can we help you?" asked Knox.

"I hope so. Your officers let us in but wouldn't tell us what's going on."

"Most of them don't know what's going on," said Knox.

"Hell, we don't know much ourselves," added Muney.

The men held out their badges and introduced themselves —Special Agents Erkhart and Mollerman, FBI.

"Feds? What does this old la—"

"Who wants coffee and bagels?" announced a cheerful voice from the doorway.

Erkhart and Mollerman turned wide eyes on the young officer nudging his way between them.

"Son of a bitch!" cried Muney. "Does it look like we're here for a goddamn picnic, deputy?"

"Cool it, Terrence," muttered Knox. "I doubt the kid's acting on his own authority. Who sent you, Officer, uh... Radabaugh?"

The officer grimaced at Muney, then shoved his way to the table. He set down a bag packed with bagels and another with a 96-ounce box of coffee and several paper cups. Shrugging, he gazed around the apartment and resumed his pleasant disposition. "It was Lieutenant Valcourt. When he heard the address, he said his gran used to live around here. Said this bagel shop down the block, Huntsman's, has 'the best damn cuppa joe and sourdough bagel in all five boroughs.' Since it seemed like you're gonna be here all day, he called in the order and sent me round to deliver it. I'm just the errand boy, detective."

Innocently holding up his hands, Officer Radabaugh sneered at Muney. In an attempt to see over the detectives' shoulders, Radabaugh stood on his tiptoes and extended his neck. As the sun rose higher, it found its way in through Mrs Cazares's bedroom window, giving off an eerie red glow.

"Alright, that'll be enough, Radabaugh," said Knox, stepping forward to shove him out. "Pass our thanks along to the lieutenant. Now, go and help them out on the street."

Muney glared at the departing smart-ass deputy while Knox opened the paper bag to smell the bagels. His eyebrows rose as he inhaled, then he smirked and offered the bag to the special agents.

"No thanks," said Mollerman.

"You sure?" asked Knox. "He wasn't kidding. Smell that?"

Mollerman shook his head. "Would you mind informing us about what you got here?"

Now Erkhart was stepping into the apartment, peering over their shoulders just like Radabaugh. Knox stepped between him and Mrs Cazares's bedroom, holding out the bag of bagels.

"Hang on a minute," said Muney. "Who called the feds already? We've been here less than an hour ourselves. What's this got to do with you?"

Erkhart and Mollerman shared a look and shrugged. "Actually, our business is unrelated."

"Then why don't you head on out of here?" suggested Knox, finally setting down the bag. "Get on with your business and leave us to ours. As far as we can tell, the daughter came home to get back at mommy for giving her a few too many beatings as a girl. Not sure how that ties into the Asian fellow upstairs yet, but..."

"Upstairs? Another homicide?"

Detective Muney nodded. "The superintendent says his name was Kevin Park. Used to go to NYU. Ever since he graduated, he's had trouble paying rent. That's all we know so far."

"Either of you happen to read Korean?" asked Knox.

"Korean?" said Erkhart in mild shock. He stared at his partner, then took a pad out of his pocket, flipping through it. He appeared to find what he was looking for and nodded his head. "What about Korean?"

"The boy upstairs, Kevin Park."

"He's Korean?"

Knox nodded and moved the bags around the table, searching for Park's phone. He found it and was about to show the agents the gory photograph. "He was clutching his phone and the murder weapon was—"

"Now, just hold on," interrupted Mollerman. "I'd like to take this one step at a time. We're already getting a bit twisted here. This is apartment 303, isn't it?" he asked, turning around to double-check the number on the door.

"That's right," answered Muney.

"Then, I take it Carolynn Cazares is...indisposed?" Erkhart asked.

"Permanently," Knox said with a sigh. "Why?"

"And you think the daughter did it?" asked Mollerman.

"Best guess we have at this point," nodded Muney. "Like I said, we haven't been here long ourselves. A couple of neighbors said Mrs Cazares had been...having dreams."

"I see," said Mollerman. The four men gazed at each other awkwardly for a few seconds. Then, Mollerman cleared his throat and turned to his partner. "You want to tell them?"

"Alright," said Erkhart. "Well, we received a call from the Cincinnati field office early this morning. They asked us to come here and inform Carolynn Cazares that her daughter, Julieta Cazares, was murdered last night."

"Jesus..." muttered Muney.

"What in the hell's going on around here?" Knox threw his arms up. "What happened?"

"She was found at an Exxon station about seventy-five miles east of Cincinnati. She'd been attacked in the restroom with a piece of glass from a broken mirror."

Detectives Knox and Muney shared a grim look.

"And that's not all," added Mollerman. "Down the road, they found three more bodies and evidence of a fourth. Some kind of massacre, by the sound of it, and also a hit-and-run. They think a body was hit and dragged, but there's no sign of the body. Only a necktie and a wallet. They're searching the surrounding field and checking out the local hospitals but haven't come up with anything yet. Strange thing is, everything inside the wallet is in Korean. ID card, driver's license, cash, credit cards. They've done a cursory check with immigration, and there's no record of this individual ever entering the country, let alone an explanation for what he was doing on some desolate country road in Ohio. All they got is a road full of blood and some flesh and skull fragments in the grill of an abandoned car."

"And the massacre?" asked Muney.

"Three cars," said Erkhart. "One driver missing, a Maggie Garrick out of Maryland. Two men, both of whom have yet to be identified. Neither seems to have been carrying identification, and their bodies are...well, beyond recognition. It's unclear whether the third car had anything to do with them, but she's the prime suspect for Julieta Cazares. A woman named Irene Marquardt. Ran out of gas. She was found in her driver's seat with a broken mirror shard lodged in her neck.

Came from the same mirror in the Exxon restroom that was used to kill Ms Cazares."

Detective Knox shook his head and let out a deep breath. Muney's angst appeared to have simmered, and he frowned in silent contemplation. Knox nudged Muney aside and waved the special agents into Mrs Cazares's bedroom.

"That all sounds a little too familiar for comfort," said Knox. "See for yourselves. No broken mirror here. No broken anything, in fact. Pretty sure the murder weapon is upstairs in the chest of the other victim. Haven't a clue how they're related. We need to find someone who speaks Korean."

"How's a translator going to help?" asked Mollerman.

As Erkhart went toward the bedroom, Knox held up the smartphone for Mollerman. The agent squinted and held his breath as he tried to make sense of what he was looking at. The Asian woman in the photo appeared to have been beaten, bruised, punctured, and gnawed to within an inch of her life, but the fatal blow was almost certainly still embedded in her chest.

"What the fuck is that?" said Mollerman. "Is that a...decapitated goat's head? Who the hell is s—"

"Holy shit..." muttered Erkhart, cutting off Mollerman and drawing him into the bedroom.

"Where the hell is her throat?" asked Mollerman.

"Damned if we know," said Muney. "Pretty sure it's not in here, though."

After a few minutes, Erkhart and Mollerman emerged from the bedroom.

"Looks like we've all got a lot of work ahead of us," said Erkhart. "Maybe we'll take you up on that coffee after all."

"Got any everything bagels in there?" asked Mollerman.

THE LAW AND THE PROPHETS

"Hey… Hey, wake up. Wake up. It's okay. You're safe."

"What? What happened? Where am I?"

"You're still in the car. Everything's alright. You drifted off about two hours ago."

"…"

"Don't look at me like that. You're creeping me out. Don't you… Don't you remember me?"

"No, I do. I do. It's just…another one of those dreams."

"It sounded pretty bad. You were… You've had dreams like that before?"

"I'm still with you? You're the one who picked me up near Indianapolis?"

"That's right."

"Why didn't you kick me out yet?"

"What? I… Why would I?"

"Where are we?"

"Somewhere in Ohio. Middle of nowhere."

"Look, I want to thank you for, you know, picking me up and everything. It hasn't been easy catching rides. You don't need to feel, like, obligated to keep driving me or anything."

"I've got no problem with some company on the road. Besides, we're heading in the same direction. We gotta help one another out."

"What's that supposed to mean?"

"Just that. People should help one another. Whether it's a few bucks or emotional support. Or a lift across the country."

"I'm not gonna blow you or anything like that."

"No, that's not... That's not what I meant. I just meant...I'm glad to help out. That's all. Relax. But, are you alright?"

"I'm fine."

"You sure? You didn't sound like it when you were asleep."

"Yeah, maybe... I don't know."

"You have these dreams often?"

"Yeah."

"What are they about? Sometimes it helps to talk about them. Get them out in the open."

"I know it does. But why do you care? All the other drivers who saw me dreaming like that just threw me out. Hey! What the fuck are you laughing about?"

"Nothing! I swear! I just...I already told you why. I like to help people. That's it. And I'm interested."

"Really?"

"You've really had a rough time traveling the highways, huh?"

"Yeah, but it's not that. It's the nightmares."

"Tell me."

"They started a few months back. Just regular bad dreams at first. This, like, ghoulish entity would whisper to me from the shadows, occasionally reaching its freakishly long arm out to caress me with nails like bear claws. After a few weeks, those garbled whispers cleared up into something that resembled sensible speech. Its words had the effect of memories, reminding me of things I ran away from more than fifteen years ago. Shit, I was a teenager. Just a kid, really. Streetwise, maybe, but without any real experience. I learned a lot of hard lessons those first couple of years on my own."

"Like what?"

"How to stand up for myself, for one. That sure would have come in handy back home when my mom was calling me a useless whore and knocking me around. I also learned how important it is to have people you can depend on when things go wrong. Figured out how to be assertive to get what I want. The most important one, though...never mind. It's dumb."

"I doubt that. Just tell me."

"You know, it's like that old saying...treat people with kindness and they'll treat you the same. It's not always true, of course. But it works more often than I thought it would—even when you're homeless and haven't showered in a week."

"That's not dumb."

"No, I guess not. But it's common sense. Once I realized it, I thought I was so stupid because it seems so obvious, and people always say things like that. Isn't it in the Bible?"

"Sure is. Matthew, chapter seven, verse twelve. It's called the Golden Rule."

"What? You a Bible thumper or something?"

"No, no. Nothing like that. My mom is, so I had to study all that stuff in Sunday School. But now...I go to church sometimes."

"So you're a believer?"

"Yes... Aren't you?"

"Not in anything like that. God or the word of Jesus. After struggling on my own for a while and figuring things out, I did start to believe in something. A force of good, I guess. The positive energy of the universe. Maybe it's all the same thing. Now, though...I don't know anymore. These nightmares have made me question everything I used to know. I still believe in all that hippy stuff, for the most part. Peace and love and karma. To each his own and take care of your spirit. But I've been reminded that there's more to it than that. For every yin, there's a yang."

"What?"

"I mean, nothing exists in isolation. If there's good in the world, then there must be bad, too, existing right alongside it. Balance. In nature, it all works out. We think of it as harmony. But when people get involved, bringing their petty grievances and hidden desires and sick manias into the picture, it doesn't work out so pretty, does it? It just fucks with the natural order."

"I see what you mean. Justice, fairness, equality—things like that? Misused and tossed out the window."

"Right."

"Where'd you say you were coming from again?"

"I've been in Washington about seven years now."

"Washington is beautiful. My brother and his wife live in Seattle."

"I was closer to Olympia. Salt Lake, before that. Tucson and Vegas, too. A couple of years in each."

"Why not California?"

"I tried. Couldn't stand it."

"Will you go back to Olympia?"

"Why?"

"Because...well, what you said shortly after you hopped in made it sound like you have no plans to. But you've got no luggage."

"..."

"It's none of my business. I know. But you seem like a smart woman, and nice, so—"

"Nice..."

"I didn't mean to—"

"No, it's alright. Really. It's kind of you to say that. I don't know about smart, but I have certainly tried to be nice. I struggled a lot in the Southwest, but with the help of some good friends, I found a new mindset in Washington. Gave me some much-needed perspective. I was able to flip my chaotic life into something...worth the effort. Stopped running with rough crowds. Stopped attaching myself to abusive assholes. Stopped using. I've been sober ever since I stepped across the Washington state line. Still am. Had a couple of close calls hitchhiking these past few weeks. Got picked up by a few truck drivers. One of them drank on the road, the other had a stash of meth he sells at truck stops. Rode through Wyoming in a van with a group of college stoners, like, real Scooby-Doo shit. Cutting through the Indian reservations was the worst. There's too much of everything harmful there. Those people have to be as strong as mountains. And coming through Iowa was like making my way through an opiate factory. But I've been firm."

"You should be proud of yourself."

"When I left last month, I was worried about my addictions. But after a month on the road, I don't have any desire for that stuff. Not because I don't want it, but because I'm afraid."

"Afraid to fall back into the pit of addiction. My brother—"

"No, not that. Afraid it'll make the nightmares worse."

"It's taken you a month to get from Washington to Ohio?"

"Crazy, isn't it? People are wary of picking up hitchhikers these days. It only took me a week to get out West when I ran away. Coast to coast. Now, nine cars out of ten speed by, and the one that does pick me up is almost always local. They take me to the nearest town, and that's it. The few that took me farther always...well, they respectfully kicked me out."

"Can I ask why?"

"I told you. The nightmares."

"..."

"Do you know it?"

"Know what?"

"That Bible verse."

"I think so. Let me see...uh... *'In everything, whatsoever you would have men do to you, you must do so to them, for this sums up the Law and the Prophets.'* Something like that. Then it goes on, *'Follow thus and enter the gate straight, for wide is the gate and broad is the way that leads toward destruction. Many enter thus, crooked and lost, because straight is the gate, and narrow is the way that leads unto life, and few can find the way.'"*

"The Law and the Prophets... What's that supposed to mean?"

"I think it has to do with trusting that God speaks through men."

"And women."

"Yes, and women. Sorry."

"But there's a counterpoint to that. The yin and yang. The balance."

"What do you mean?"

"Well, when other people treat you a certain way, it sort of...rubs off. Doesn't matter if they treat you good or bad. Before, you called me nice. And I know I am, but that's because I try to be. I have to really try. Even all these years later, the things my mother did to me as a child—the way she spoke to me, the names she called me, the times she pushed me down the stairs or cut my hair or chipped my tooth—that way of acting still seems natural to me. It takes more effort than I'd like to admit to keep those things buried. I thought I'd done it, but then the nightmares started. Dug it all right back up again. I'm more like my mother than I thought. I'm just like her."

"Do you want to talk about the nightmares?"

"..."

"You don't have to if you don't want to."

"I do want to. You're right, it helps. But the other drivers...a few of them asked, too. Then they...you know. You won't want to hear about them. Believe me."

"Maybe. But I have to admit, you've made me curious."

"I already told you about them."

"A little. Everyone has nightmares sometimes, but they're

usually not enough to send someone hitchhiking across the country. There's more to your story."

"Yeah, I sound crazy and probably am."

"I don't think that, but…"

"Feels like I am."

"So, what are they about?"

"Hey. Do you see that? Way up ahead."

"Where? I don't see anything…"

"It's hard to make out. It's so dark. No, look up. Above the road. Is that smoke?"

"Smoke? Then where's the fire? I don't see any flames. It looks thicker than smoke, anyhow. Opaque. Like a black hot air balloon or—"

"It's gone."

"Yeah…"

"How did it move so fast?"

"Where the hell did it go?"

"See, I really am crazy."

"If you are, then so am I. I saw it, too."

"But what was it?"

"It might have been a tornado. Sometimes, they'll form but never touch down. Just sort of spin in the sky for a while and then break apart."

"Really? Could it come back?"

"I don't know…"

"…"

"So?"

"What?"

"Your nightmares?"

"Right. Well, like I already told you, they started out as meaningless whispers. Creepy as hell, but at least they weren't saying anything I could understand. When the words began to take on a form, it felt like being strapped down in a chair—an electric chair or something—and this thing would crawl right up to me, standing over me, pawing and whispering and…and touching me, licking me, and… But that wasn't even the worst part. Every time it touched me, it felt like my mother. Slapping, scratching, throwing things at me. Pulling my hair. It looked like a…I don't know…like a man made out of coal. Always smoldering and smoking, you know? When he moved, cracks would form on the outer layer, revealing red-hot insides. Like lava. It had horns, a beard on its chin, a long face—"

"Like…the devil?"

"I don't know. More like an animal. It walked on four legs, but sometimes it stood upright. That's not the point, though. It didn't matter how it looked—it smelled like my mother. Its entire purpose was to remind me of all the abuse I've spent my life running from. Trying to forget. And it worked. I wake from the nightmares feeling like a piece of shit, just like I felt as a kid. She's in my nostrils. I can taste her cigarettes and feel the scars where she burned me. My stomach cramps, my head pounds, my chest aches, just like they always used to after she finished. Embarrassment and shame follow me out of bed, out into the world…and all I want to do is take it out on someone. I've shouted at people in the streets, called store clerks awful names, shoved people out of my way for no reason, and damaged property. It's not like me to do these things—not since I was a runaway delinquent acting out—but that thing in the nightmares has planted this fear and resentment in me, and I just have to… I have to let it out in tiny spurts, or I'll completely lose control."

"Relax, it's okay. Relax. Then, if you're heading to New York, I assume that's where you're from? Still got family there? Going to get some help?"

"*Hmph…* No."

"Did something happen back in Olympia?"

"No."

"Just looking for a change?"

"No."

"You want to...confront your mother, don't you?"

"..."

"Sorry, sorry. None of my business."

"Look at that..."

"What?"

"Those two cars up ahead. They're not moving."

"You're right. What the hell...?"

"The doors are open. Do you think something happ—*Look out!*"

"Shit! I just missed it. Thanks for... Was that a fucking person? Lying in the middle of the road?"

"I don't think... It was a body, but I don't think he was alive. Didn't you see his neck?"

"Oh my God... Are you seeing this?"

"Is it oil?"

"I don't think so. Look, there. On the shoulder."

"Oh... This feels like one of my nightmares..."

"Those are fucking body parts."

"Don't you think we should stop? And help them?"

"Help who? There's no one here! They're all dead!"

"Maybe they did that to each other."

"How? Do you really think that?"

"No."

"I don't even want to know who—or what—could do that. That body, it had no... It's limbs were strewn... There was no head..."

"I saw it... I saw the head. It was—"

"No, don't. I don't think I want to know. I just want to get away..."

"..."

"..."

"Look, I want to answer your question. I have to. But I need to be honest."

"What question? All I can think about is that fucking bloodbath we just drove through. In the middle of the road! Where are we? Where's my phone? I need to call someone..."

"In the nightmares, the whispers, they reminded me about my mother because...they were telling me...telling me..."

"What?"

"Telling me to return the favor. That thing that comes to me in the nightmares, it wants me to go home, back to her..."

"To tell her off? To forgive her? Hey, do you see my phone on the floor there? Or maybe it slid under the seat. I can't find it..."

"Forgive? Haven't you heard anything I said? Not forgiveness. Retribution. Your mind is too deep in the word of Jesus to see the real world, isn't it? It wants me to kill her. It demands it."

"..."

"You asked. I told you you wouldn't want to know—*Hey! Watch the road!*"

"Jesus! What's going on around here? What the hell was that?"

"It looked like a...a..."

"A goat? This is insane. Since when do wild goats roam around Ohio?"

"What's that light up ahead?"

"Looks like a gas station. I think we'd better stop and..."

"Yeah..."

"So, are you...are you really planning to murder your mother?"

"I don't want to! I have to! If I don't, the nightmares will continue. It told me so. This is the only way. I told you. It's crazy. I'm crazy. I know it. I know how it sounds. But these... they're not just nightmares. They're real. If I don't, then... I can't! I can't! I can't even think about what will happen if I don't. Everything I've been through, everything I've built from the shit of a life she gave me. I don't deserve any of this. But she does. She deserves the nightmares, not me."

"But there are other w—"

"No! There's no other way!"

"..."

"..."

"It's an Exxon. They're open. Why don't you...go inside and...do you have money?"

"Do you want something?"

"No, I..."

"You're respectfully kicking me out, aren't you?"

"I'm sorry, Julieta. I... Morally, I just can't. I can't be a part of this. This is not the sort of help I meant. If I carry you any closer to committing a murder—a matricide—I'll never be able to forgive myself. The rest of my life will be torture. And after what we've just seen, I don't know...that kind of hellish torment seems a whole lot more real..."

"It's alright. I knew you would ask me to get out eventually. I shouldn't have told you. Should have known you'd be like all the others. I guess I just...

"What?"

"I was hoping someone might be able to talk me out of it. Or take me someplace. Or do something to stop me from thinking this is the only way. You tried. And I'm grateful for that, but I don't think anyone can help. You know that. You can hear it in my voice. It's already wormed into me too deep, hasn't it? Anything you say or do, anywhere you take me, it won't matter. I'll just go to sleep and have another one of those nightmares. Then I'll wake up and keep heading to New York. To mother. I'll have to."

"..."

"Don't worry. I've got some money. I could use a bathroom break and a wash anyway. Thanks for bringing me this far. I'll be alright here. Someone else will come along. Maybe I'll learn to keep my mouth shut. I'll tell the clerk to call the police about that mess back on the road. You just drive safe. And thanks for listening, John. Really. Thank you. You were right. Talking about it really did make me feel better. A lot better. I've even got that song stuck in my head."

"What song?"

"You know, after the dwarfs have been in the mines all day, digging up their diamonds or whatever. *Heigh ho, heigh ho...*"

"*It's home from work we go...* Seems like a strange choice."

"It's not a choice. I used to watch that movie a lot as a little girl. None of it is a choice."

"I hope things work out for you. I really do. You're too nice to throw your life away like this. Remember the Law and the Prophets."

"How could I forget? They're telling me what to do. Thanks again. So long."

ABOUT THE AUTHOR

Anton Brinza was born in 1983 in Milwaukee, Wisconsin. He is the author of the horror series *The EORYX Saga* and the non-horror novel *Strike, Stay Your Hand*. When he is not writing he can generally be found consuming horrors, playing the drums, or crafting homemade hot sauce. He lives with his wife in South Korea.